HOW TO BATTLE GIANT MONSTERS WITH A DRUNK SPACE NINJA

THE ADVENTURES OF DUKE LAGRANGE, BOOK IV

JAY KEY

To Lola and Little H...

And Earth...you're welcome.

LAFAYETTE "DUKE" LAGRANGE

CHAPTER 1

YOU WOULDN'T UNDERSTAND

THE JAIL WASN'T UNFAMILIAR TO her. She had been there once before, two cycles ago, during the Tournament of the Shield of the Colossal Calamari, but had been contently on the bar-less side of the enclosure during that visit. Time had passed incredibly slowly for Mazilda Cloax since then, as it typically does in the Chief Interrogator General of Psitakki's chamber of horror. The torture had been exceptionally tough on the assassin—not because of the menacing tools that the Chief Interrogator employed (and they *were* menacing) but because he was torturing her for the sheer fun of it. She had no special information that would help those who claimed to be the "good guys" of the universe; she held no secrets nor blueprints for a weapon of galactic destruction. Had she possessed something of value, she could have willed herself through even the most heinous and painful torture sessions to prevent that asset from being handed over to the enemy; but Mazilda was being poked, prodded, and mutilated because her captor liked it. Then again, Mazilda wasn't overly surprised because she *had* been instrumental in the near collapse of the universe during the Great LePaco War. That type of crime usually came with some level of pain. Nevertheless, the Chief Interrogator General was breaking her.

"How's my favorite patient today?" the brutish Psitakki asked, lumbering towards the cell. "It's been two full cycles. You can make this pain stop, you know. All you have to do is apologize. You apologize, you get to rot away in here in peace."

"He was right," Mazilda replied, her mouth gummy. It hurt to speak; her words were shards of glass tumbling down her sticky esophagus. "LePaco *was* right."

"So you say. In fact, you say that every day. Same thing. Over and over. What does it mean? Right about what?" asked the Inspector. His voice seemed even more disinterested than usual. He turned around and sauntered to the corner of the room, where a small table stood. On the table was a metallic box, the lid opened, revealing a mishmash of pain-inducing tools.

"You wouldn't understand," snarled Mazilda.

The Inspector did not respond. He held up an especially pointy instrument against a flickering light mounted on the wall. He grabbed a file specifically designed to attach to the hook that constituted one of his hands and sharpened the point even more, blowing off the resulting fragments with a loud puff of air. He wiped the object on his sleeve.

"I think we'll do a bit of this today, if that's okay with you," he bellowed, holding up the recently sharpened tool, without turning around. "When Grozzel dropped you off here after the war and said I had carte blanche in my choice of entertainment, I thought I had died and gone to see the Colossal Calamari in the sky."

"Thanks. Can't wait."

"So what did you mean by 'he was right'?" asked the Psitakki.

Mazilda's violet eyebrows raised in unison. She ran her hands through the ridge of purple hair that extended down the middle of her cranium. Despite the torture and horrid conditions in the prison, her hair remained as electric and vibrant as when she was captured.

"You wouldn't understand. You *couldn't* understand," she huffed and slunk back down against the far wall of her cage.

The hideous, half-deformed face of the Psitakki torture aficionado turned to Mazilda. His upper lip, including tentacles, twisted and shriveled by time, raised to reveal what Mazilda could only guess constituted a smile. "Try me."

This is a waste of time, thought Mazilda.

"Come on, try me," repeated the Chief Interrogator General.

"Fine," Mazilda acquiesced.

The Psitakki mumbled something. Mazilda thought it was something along the lines of "this should be good."

Total waste of time, Mazilda reiterated to herself.

"I'm all ears, love," he said, pointing his hooked appendage at the side of his head.

"Fine. I know you probably think that Admiral LePaco was just a crazed lunatic, bent on universal domination, right?"

"I don't think of Admiral LePaco much at all. Never really concerned myself with *why* he was trying to reduce existence to rubble. Just glad he was stopped. Just glad *you* were stopped."

The assassin rolled her eyes. "I knew you wouldn't understand. But whatever. So, he wasn't trying to reduce existence to rubble. Quite the contrary."

"Oh yeah?" replied the Inspector.

"He was trying to create an orderly universe. One governed by a single all-powerful entity."

"And I'm guessing he was that 'all-powerful entity'?" asked the Psitakki.

"Yes, until he built his government up. That's what the Four I's were hired to do. And they were doing a great job."

"But why? Everything seemed pretty good here on Psitakki. I didn't feel that we needed some almighty singularity to restore balance or bring us out of an unfathomable chaos."

"See, I knew you wouldn't understand," pouted Mazilda.

"Educate me, then," countered the Inspector. "I'm not going anywhere. You definitely aren't going anywhere. I have a pretty impressive record when it comes to attempted escapes, in that they don't ever work. Ever."

"What about Duke LaGrange?" Mazilda quipped.

"That was a technicality. A loophole that only reveals itself every ten thousand cycles," he shouted back.

Sensitive, much? Mazilda mused.

"Anyway, weren't you about to tell me why we needed a savior like Admiral LePaco?" asked the Interrogator, changing the subject.

"The universe is big, right? Very big. Infinitely big."

"Yes. So?"

"But it's not," smirked Mazilda.

"It's not big?" the brute replied, turning around to face Mazilda. "You sure about that?"

"No, it *is* big. But it's not *infinitely big*. That was a lie being used by nearly all sentient beings to make it seem like a fruitless endeavor to establish a single unifying body."

"So, you're saying that the same falsehood is being carried on by nearly every single evolved race across the cosmos?" asked the Psitakki, obviously confused.

"Yes."

"But...how? And more importantly...why?"

"The 'why' is easy. The architect of the scam had an interest in keeping us all disorganized. If we were in chaos, we could never mount any sort of offensive."

"Against what?"

"The other dimension," Mazilda responded, matter-of-factly.

The Chief Interrogator General audibly sighed and turned back around and started to sharpen more of his torture instruments.

"I'm serious," pleaded Mazilda. "Think about it. There was a thing in this universe that was around from the beginning, when almost every civilization was being born. That thing would have been able to keep us blindfolded and fighting against each other, against the idea of a strong unified universe."

"I have a feeling I know what you're going to say, and I will preempt it by saying that you are, in fact, insane," the Psitakki said.

Mazilda leapt to her feet and approached the bars of the cage. Her belly burned, her molars ground on each other. "Queen Joe was our enemy. *Is* our enemy. It wasn't Admiral LePaco," she exclaimed with a smile. "She wasn't sent here to watch the artifacts, she was sent here to protect her dimension—whether by destroying us or making us unable to become significant opposition. The Admiral was close to taking her out and establishing a powerful, organized universe. Then, it would have been us that could have invaded dimensions and be the conquerors...not the conquered."

"There it is," said the Interrogator. "I knew it would come out eventually. The crazy always surfaces if you let it talk long enough. First off, the Queen is gone."

"No she's not," interrupted Mazilda.

"The Queen is gone. And it seems like LePaco wanted us organized so we could go invade some dimensions that haven't done anything to us. That's—"

"They sent Joe here to destroy us!" Mazilda exclaimed. *How is he not getting this?*

The Chief Interrogator General pivoted and headed towards Mazilda. He held aloft the instrument that he had been sharpening. "I have a few new techniques that we're going to try today. It won't feel good, but maybe it will knock some of the insanity out of you."

The Psitakki reached for the cell door but stopped suddenly. He let out a painful groan. He looked down; blood covered his midsection. He looked up and locked eyes with Mazilda.

"You insane—"

He fell over. Dead.

Behind him stood a shapely figure in a cloak and hood, not too dissimilar from the one Mazilda typically wore. The arm that extended from the opening in the front of the cloak was the color of sun-bleached sand, ending in a humanoid hand with slender fingers and perfectly manicured nails. It held a pulse pistol; the design was nothing that Mazilda had seen before in her many travels, and that was saying a lot. Mazilda remained motionless.

The pulse pistol discharged a second time. Mazilda instinctively jumped back to avoid the explosion. The shot was not aimed at her; instead, it blew the door lock into a mound of unrecognizable scrap metal. The door slowly and inelegantly swung open.

"Who are—"

"Shut up, Mazilda Cloax," the robed figure said, cutting her off. The voice was stern but melodic. "Your services have been requested."

"By who—"

"There's a ship in the dock behind the arena. Do you know where that is?"

"Yes. But—"

"The ship sports a simple insignia on the front: a circle with a ring of fire on its edges."

"A sun?"

"You call it a sun, I call it a circle with a ring of fire on its edges. Are you really wasting time on questions like this? You have much to learn, Mazilda Cloax. Be there by the time the sun goes down or you will be stuck here on Psitakki."

Or do you mean when the circle with a ring of fire on its edges goes down? Mazilda quipped internally.

"And you don't want to be stuck on this planet once they realize that you killed the Chief Interrogator General," continued the mysterious gunman. "I hope to see you again."

The cloaked figure exited the room in a flash.

Mazilda cautiously exited her cell. She inhaled deeply.

Freedom tastes good. She stumbled over the Interrogator's lifeless corpse before steadying herself.

"Say hi to the Colossal Calamari in the sky for me."

CHAPTER 2

STARSPLITTER

"UPDATES?" BELTED MAZILDA CLOAX ACROSS the bridge of the *Starsplitter*. It was one of the speediest ships in the private collection of the late Admiral LePaco. Upon the would-be cosmic overlord's death at the hands of bounty hunter Duke LaGrange, his seemingly endless inventory of war machines and death-inducing toys was ravaged by the remnants of his once powerful military. The *Starsplitter* was quickly snatched up by a member of the defunct Intergalactic Infrastructure Improvement, Incorporated, known simply as the Four I's. That employee was Redd Warwick, and he had the very prestigious title of Director of Strategic Initiatives and Integrated Planning Operations. Mazilda didn't think much of Redd—he was too squishy and whiny for her liking—but she also knew one important key fact about him that had helped her gain ownership of the *Starsplitter*—he had a big ol' crush on her.

"Updates?" she repeated.

"The last of the force in this sector has joined us, Captain," squeaked Redd Warwick. "There were more Four I's legions out there than I thought. It's not LePacosized anymore but it's a pretty darn good force, especially when you count the Jungafallowians and the other mercenaries."

"Good job," said Mazilda.

"Why thank you, Captain. Your praise humbles me," Warwick replied, bowing repeatedly.

Such a squirrely little bastard, thought Mazilda. *But hey, all it took was a wink and an extended hug to get a ship from him; maybe he's useful for something.*

"Now that we have enough ships to invade most any planet, are you going to tell us what we're doing? Where we're going?" asked a Tardasian male named Rozz. "I didn't recognize the coordinates that you gave the portal operator on our last jump."

Rozz, like most Tardasians, was fat. Not husky or heavyset or big-boned. He was fat. Blubbery, jiggly, bulbous. Fat. But, like most Tardasians, he was also cunning. Rozz chose to use his elevated intelligence on the mechanics of combat and holistic military strategy; he knew a hundred ways to blow something up and a thousand ways to sneak up on that thing *to* blow it up. But he likely had never thrown a punch or dodged a bullet in his life. Mazilda thought he was perfect for an Operations Officer, whatever that meant.

"Yes, pretty soon. Just simmer down," she said in a soft yet commanding voice.

"Come on, Mazilda," growled a Jungafallowian. "If I'm going to have my brethren attack something, I want to know what it is first."

Though they suffered heavy losses in the war, the Jungafallowians probably fared the best of LePaco's forces. They were skilled in battle, be it in their ships or on the ground, and were just generally a hearty breed. Darfol-Chell was an especially nasty one; scarred and weathered from far too many skirmishes, even for a Jungafallowian. But Mazilda knew that the two-headed reptiloids hated answering to non-Jungas; they barely trusted LePaco, after all. So Darfol-Chell was a necessary conduit to mobilize the xenophobic brutes. He had spent much time in the Trampling Death Robots Fan Club & Attack Squad, Jungafallow III Chapter, under the very respected but now very dead Prince Korzo-Tapor; so he knew how to kill things effectively.

"They want to know. I want to know," one of Darfol-Chell's heads snarled. "We're concerned because you're being so secretive about this mission."

"Yeah," Rozz concurred.

"Calm down. If Mazilda isn't telling you something, there's a good reason for it," interjected Redd. "She's our leader and the best leader in the—"

"Shut up, weasel," hissed the Darfol head as it twisted to the left and invaded the personal space of the former Four I's officer. "Go back to cleaning the floor or something useful."

Warwick's head immediately dropped. He stepped two paces back. The Jungafallowian huffed. Rozz rolled his eyes.

He is a weasel, thought Mazilda.

"Do you have anything to ask, Az? Since I'm apparently fielding questions, we might as well get them all out in the open," Mazilda snarked.

"Why are you asking the robot?" bellowed the Chell head. "He's just going to agree with you. I'm sure you programmed him that way."

"He's not a robot—" began Mazilda.

"I'm a cyborg," Az said, finishing her thought. His voice was calm, almost soothing, but dripping in evil. It was clear that Az had done a lot of harm to a lot of beings in his life.

He even gave Mazilda the chills, and she had spent two cycles in the torture chamber of the Psitakki Chief Interrogator General. "I do my own thinking. And I'd venture a guess that an eighth of my brain power is more than triple the combined capacity of your two."

The grizzled Jungafallowian shook both his heads. The corner of Az's lip turned upward. His mouth was entirely organic, as was most of his head, outside of a large circular area that extended from the left side of his cranium, encompassing his eye and ear. The metallic surface was sleek, with no rivets or noticeable welding, and had two tubes that stretched to a similar metallic surface on his back. He was clearly a premium model of cyborg.

"I hate robots," muttered the Jungafallowian.

"No, Mazilda, I don't have any questions. I assume that wherever we are going, I get to kill people. And for that killing, I'll get paid. I assume that, if this plan had changed, I would have been notified."

"You are very correct, Az. When your services are needed, you will know it. I will send for you personally."

"And could my victims include a few bounty hunters? I will kill *them* for free, you know."

"I will do my best, Az. I have some in mind that would be great trophies on your wall."

The cyborg raised his entirely mechanical left arm and saluted Mazilda, bowed, and walked towards the innards of the ship. But not without a slight brushing of shoulders with both Darfol-Chell and Rozz.

"Why did you let that mercenary join our crew?" asked Rozz.

"Because he's one of the best in the universe at doing bad things," she answered firmly. "Like real bad things. If I need to drop someone off in the middle of a swamp on Gordget to go and assassinate an exiled Mega-Troll in hiding, guarded by a battalion of Hausen-Ra, are *you* going to volunteer?"

"Well, that's not really my strength..." Rozz's sloped forehead wrinkled as he slunk behind Darfol-Chell.

"How about you, big guy?" Mazilda said.

"Sure, I'm not scared of anything," proclaimed the Darfol head. "Not even a Mega-Troll in a marsh surrounded by skeleton warriors."

"I don't doubt that but, no offense, you aren't exactly qualified for a stealth kill mission."

Both the Darfol and Chell heads' lips flared, exposing gnarly teeth.

He knows I'm right, thought Mazilda.

"So that's why he's on our team," she continued. "When we inevitably have a special chore that needs a special type of being with special skills, Az will handle it. Plus, he's our only link to the mercenaries who we've recruited. They weren't exactly chomping at the bit to join us after our last showing on Kelt. Az convinced them that it would be well worth their time."

"Well, I still don't like robots," muttered the Jungafallowian.

Mazilda didn't acknowledge the hulking alien. She turned to face the forward screen on the bridge. "Zoom in," she barked at the former Four I's officer piloting the ship. "Let's show these eager boys where we're heading."

Mazilda could feel Darfol-Chell and Redd Warwick standing behind her. She could smell Rozz.

"Gentlemen," she began. "That's our target. That's the planet we're going to take over."

"You've got to be kidding me," shouted the Taradasian.

Darfol-Chell exhaled noisily, said something under his breath, and headed to the back of the ship.

Well, he's not a happy camper, concluded Mazilda.

"Are you sure, Captain?" asked Warwick. "I trust your judgment. I will follow you anywhere, but—"

"Yes, I'm sure, Redd. Go let Az know. You and Rozz organize the war room, we have an attack to plan."

On the view screen, nestled against the infinite black of space, was a strange little planet. It looked almost tranquil from this distance, but Mazilda knew that it was quite possibly the most unpredictable, volatile, and dangerous place in the known universe—and also one of the most important in the advancement of intergalactic discovery and contact. Her mission was simple. Take over the one place that had never been taken over in its existence, because no one was stupid enough or brave enough to try. They did a good enough job taking over themselves. Most sentient races thought war was invented here, or at the very least, perfected.

Mazilda's gaze lingered on the wholly unassuming sphere.

"Let's stay here," she belted to the pilot, snapping out of her daze. "This should do. We should be outside of any of their scanners."

"Confirmed," responded the pilot.

"Good. Good. Just think, you'll be able to tell your friends and family that you piloted the lead ship of the force that did the unthinkable and took over Earth."

Mazilda didn't give the pilot a chance to answer, or if he did, she didn't hear it. She headed back into the interior of the ship to prepare for the invasion.

CHAPTER 3

QUEEN JOE'S

"BEER," ORDERED THE BARREL-CHESTED Neprian, the torchlight reflecting off his bald cranium. "And make it snappy."

"How about I snap your fat head off your even fatter neck?" replied the handsome Nova Texan with a twisted smile.

The Neprian paused, then let out a deep belly laugh. "Duke, I've missed you, you bastard!"

"You too, Bu'r. I was starting to wonder when you'd come back here and visit me. Shud'nut isn't that far from Dre'en. I should know, I walked it," said Duke.

"I know, I know. I've been a bad friend. But there's a lot to do down there; remember, the villagers weren't too kind to us when we liberated them from Orbius' clutches," replied Bu'r. "It's been keeping me busy. Very busy. But I couldn't go an entire cycle without seeing this place. It's the talk of Neprius. They've all been chattering; 'you have to go to Queen Joe's,' they say."

"Well, it's good to see you," replied Duke as he slid a mug of ale across the bar top and into the waiting hand of Bu'r. A bit of liquid sloshed out of the glass and onto the bar. But not as much as expected. *I'm getting better*, thought Duke.

"So what's with the name, anyways? Who's Queen Joe?" asked Bu'r.

"It's a long story."

"I'm game. I don't have to head back to Shud'nut until tomorrow morning," replied Bu'r.

"Okay, then. Think of Queen Joe...think of her as a, well..." Duke bit his bottom lip, struggling for the right description. "Think of her as a pan-dimensional visitor who predates all known life in our universe, sent here to guard some all-powerful artifacts from these shadow demons from back in her dimension. She also ran a bar—"

"Fine, LaGrange," Bu'r said, cutting him off. "If you don't want to tell me, just say so. No need to be an ass." He downed his beer in a single gulp.

"No, I'm serious—"

"How about you just get me another beer? You're a better bartender than storyteller, it seems."

"Sounds good," the bounty hunter said with a smile. He slid another mug to Bu'r; even less ale spilled this time around. "So, what do you think of the place?"

Bu'r ceased downing his drink and placed the mug back on the bar. His eyes scanned the entire establishment.

I was just looking for a simple 'yeah, not too shabby,' not some in-depth analysis, thought Duke.

"Not too shabby," replied Bu'r. "I really like it. It's homey. Charming. What's that over there? A stage?"

"It is. I plan to get some local musicians in here every once in a while. The original...the inspiration, I guess you could say...on a planet called Kelt, had a stage. So I thought, why not do the same here? Though I hope to be a bit more particular about the acts that come through here," said Duke.

"What was that place called? Queen Joe's?"

"No, Cyborg Joe's," replied the bounty hunter.

"What's a cyborg?"

"That's precisely why he didn't name it that, you over-weight imbecile," interjected a voice. It was squeaky and nasally. And the jingles and jangles of way too many trinkets and jewelry served as a backing track.

"Vern!" Bu'r shouted as he leapt from his barstool and grabbed the gaunt Neprian priest with a massive, consuming bear hug. Bu'r wrenched back, lifting the much lighter being in the air. "I didn't know you were in Dre'en! I assumed you were up north in Sansagon doing your ambassadory duties."

He released the former priest and placed him back on the firm ground. Vernglet Wip, Ambassador of the North, pulled up a barstool and sat down.

"Ja'a keeping you busy, Vern?" asked Duke.

"Yes, afraid so. Turning around the perception of an entire generation of Neprians—North and South alike—does require time and effort. It's no small task. And one that Ja'a is doing admirably."

"You have to be so proud of her, Duke," added Bu'r. "This is the first time in a long while that most folks are generally happy."

"She's a pretty impressive woman," concluded Duke as he wiped down a thin, conical glass. He emptied a burgundy liquid into the vessel and gave it to the Ambassador.

"Thanks, Duke. How much do I owe you for this wine? It's a good vintage, you know," said Vernglet.

"On the house."

Vernglet Wip nodded with a smile. "So Duke, not to be blunt and if you don't mind me asking of course, what's bothering you?" he asked.

"What do you mean?" responded the Nova Texan, halting his bar top wiping mid-rotation. "Who said anything's wrong?"

"You did," Vernglet replied matter-of-factly. "You didn't say it outright, but I can tell."

"You do seem a little less, what's the word, I'm looking for, Vern...*fun*?" Bu'r added.

"Is it because Ja'a is working a lot more? Less time together," prodded Vern.

"No! Even if that was the case, what she's doing is more important than *us*, as a couple, ya know. I mean, I do wish she was around more—I'm not crazy—but it's not bothering me," Duke countered.

"I'd miss her," Bu'r mumbled.

Duke's eyes darted to the husky Neprian, his stare trying to burrow into the face of Bu'r.

"What? I would," Bu'r added. "Just telling you the truth. Oh yeah, I need another beer."

The bounty hunter bartender obliged and sent another mug into Bu'r's hand. Not a drop spilled.

"So, then what? What is making Duke LaGrange—adventurer, trailblazer, poet, a true man of the universe—become so complacent running this quaint drinking establishment?" asked the former priest.

Duke took in a deep breath. He could feel Vernglet's stare; it was as if he was trying to dig deep into the recesses of his soul and excavate a long-buried secret. The bounty hunter exhaled.

"Quaint?" Duke replied, feigning insult.

"Stop avoiding the question," the Ambassador pressed.

"You got me, Vern. You're right, something is wrong."

The Northern Neprian inched to the edge of his barstool. His eyes widened to the point where Duke thought they might extend beyond the outer edge of his ovoid face.

"Yes?"

"I'm running low on Glyptodian Summer Ale. I only brought so much back in the *Deus*, and I can't seem to perfect the brewing process with the equipment on this rock. It's my best seller. My second quarter projections are looking a bit soft."

Vernglet leaned back on his stool and crossed his arms. He sighed dejectedly. Bu'r tried to quell a chuckle, but it slipped through his mouth.

"Just trying to help, Duke. Just trying to help," Vern replied.

Duke refilled Vernglet Wip's wine glass.

"So do you think The Green Ninja is a better name for this place? What about Duke's? No, too cliché. Maybe just simply Orb. Too nightclubby?"

CHAPTER 4

A SPATIAL POCKET

"I LOVE OUR TIME TOGETHER. I've never known anyone as beautiful as you," whispered Duke LaGrange. "But we can't tell Ja'a. Promise?"

The *Deus Ex Machina* did not respond. It was a ship, after all. Though it had done some amazing and inexplicable things in the past, carrying on a conversation with its owner was not one of them.

But it did beep.

"Got something, girl? Is this it? Did you find it?"*Man, I made that transition to doggy talk way too easily*, thought Duke.

The volume and frequency of the beep lessened dramatically and died with an elongated whine.

"False alarm. Damn," Duke said, gently patting the control panel of his ship. "Not your fault. I think I might be on a hopeless mission with this one. And I thought that one time I was in the middle of that Quibbian Erecto-varmint stampede was hopeless. That was a piece of cake compared to this."

Duke sighed. "But then again, I *did* have a ninja with me. Right, girl? Not sure Ish could even help me find a portal out here. Neprius is just destined to be isolated to the celestial boondocks."

"More of a spatial pocket," muttered a voice from seemingly out of nowhere.

Duke drew his laser revolver mid-turn and aimed it at the unannounced intruder.

The pink goopy makeup of the Blop made it hard to tell if he was startled by having a firearm at arm's length from his face. He just sort of stood there, as if he was stuck to the floor like a piece of discarded bubblegum.

"Duke, good to see you again," Blop, the Blop from Blop began. "I mean it isn't *me* per se, but rather us. Or me. Or us. Whatever is easier for you to digest."

Duke remained frozen, his finger still resting on the trigger of his pulse pistol.

"I didn't mean to startle you. I thought I gave you a heads-up. I told your ship. It said it beeped me in," the Blop explained.

So that was the beep.

"Sorry, Blop, I don't speak ship," Duke said, exhaling and lowering his gun. "How did you get in here?"

"It's of no importance. We are pretty unique beings—"

"Yes, I know," interrupted Duke. "Unique is an understatement. So 'spatial pocket,' you say?"

"Oh, Neprius. Yes. There isn't a being-made portal within a distance that's even remotely reachable without the help of a really powerful entity or an—"

"Astral anomaly," Duke said, finishing the Blop's thought. "I know all about that."

"Right, you do."

"So how'd you get here?" asked the bounty hunter.

"Blop can get anywhere, at least in this dimension. If we don't have a physical Blop in the vicinity, we have our own ways of travel. Of course, that is proprietary in nature."

"Of course," Duke responded, his eyes rolling so far back in his head that he thought he could see his cerebral cortex. "So were you just in the area, hanging out? Did you hear about our new bar, Queen Joe's? It's getting a nice buzz about town."

"No."

"Oh."

"And no, I was not in the area. I traveled here to warn you. Or to give you, how do you say it, a 'heads-up.' It's about Earth."

"Earth? What's wrong with Earth? I mean, outside of the usual?" inquired the bounty hunter. "I would have thought Earth was heading in the right direction with Ish's parents leading the rebuild. Last time I saw 'em, even the Irish and Japanese were open to cooperating with each other. What happened?"

"Your assumption is correct. Earth has, oh I'm trying my best to translate into your crude language, turned the angle. No, wait, turned the corner. Right?"

The bounty hunter nodded.

"The parents of Ishiro'shea have done an admirable job organizing a unified Earth," continued Blop. "They even gained the help of some neighboring star systems and galaxies...better than even we could have expected. And much faster."

"So what's the problem, then?" asked Duke. The Nova Texan sat down in the navigator's chair at the control panel. He lifted his legs and placed them on the panel. He began to twirl his gun on his index finger. "Seems like it's all hunky-dory."

Blop look confused. Or that's how it came across to Duke.

"The progress that they've made is in jeopardy. Serious jeopardy."

"Let me guess, some crazy nutjob thinks the gang wars shouldn't be over and they're causing a ruckus?"

"No."

"Political gamesmanship leading to an unstable coalition?"

"No."

"Close?"

"No."

"Well, then what has that odd little planet in some much 'serious jeopardy'?" asked Duke, throwing his hands up in the air.

The Blop paused. He blinked slowly. Duke wasn't sure if he was still conscious or if he was building dramatic tension. Before Duke could ask, the enigmatic creature spoke. Duke didn't like what he said.

"Mazilda Cloax."

Duke's body hunched over in the chair. A lot of thoughts raced through his head, most of them really, really bad. *How? Why?*

"Wasn't she on Psitakki?"

"She escaped. Someone helped her. The Chief Interrogator was killed," answered the Blop.

I'm not losing any sleep over that one, thought Duke.

"We don't know her accomplice," continued Blop. "Or the motivation. Or much of anything. Other than she escaped and now is leading an invasion of Earth."

"With what? With who?"

"You helped defeat LePaco, Duke, but not everyone in his almost infinite force was killed or captured. Mazilda has rallied the remaining diehards along with some mercenaries and other assorted 'not nice' people."

"Do they actually have a chance against Earth? I mean, Earth is known for one thing. Fighting. Wars. Death."

The Blop looked confused. "That's—"

"Yes, I know. That's three things," Duke cut off the alien. "My point is that this isn't Oscavia that she's trying to attack."

"I'm not sure they know she's coming. They are really focused on the rejuvenation of their planet," Blop explained. "But it's critical that she's stopped. You may not know this, but Earth is pivotal to the existence of this dimension."

"Earth?"

"Yes. I don't have time to explain but Blop agrees."

"All of you?"

"Yes, all of Blop." He nodded.

Duke stood up and walked to his captain's chair in the direct center of the *Deus'* bridge. He sat down.

"So, I have a few more questions," he stated.

"There's not enough time, Duke. We must go," the Blop replied. His voice was even-keeled and calm, but Duke knew there was a sense of urgency behind it. And for a Blop to be in a hurry, it must be pretty dire.

"I need to talk to Ja'a. I can't leave without telling her," Duke pleaded. "And if she says no, it's a no. Okay?"

"She is aligned," the Blop responded.

"What?"

"We met with her before we talked to you."

These guys are smart.

"Feel free to verify with her. She wanted me to tell you to be safe and that Bu'r is going to run the bar for a bit. He said something about possibly changing the name to Orb to get a more youthful clientele."

"That son of a bitch!" Duke shouted.

"She said that was a joke. I sure hope I delivered it correctly. We Blop don't really comprehend humor," he explained.

The bounty hunter furrowed his eyebrows. *That does sound like Ja'a.* "And how will we get there?" asked Duke.

"I will take care of that."

"Last request," said Duke.

"Yes?"

"Can we make a quick stop before we get to Earth?"

"Where to?"

"A bar," Duke replied with a grin. "I'm not going to Earth alone."

CHAPTER 5

THE FATHER'S SPEECH

THE FATHER WAS USED TO public speaking. He was used to intense brainstorming sessions. He was used to hard-hitting debate. He was not, however, used to addressing the most influential government officials on his planet. The Irish-Japanese Gang Wars prevented the need for these sorts of diplomatic gatherings. He uneasily made his way to the podium. The leaders of what he hoped would be a true unified Earth stared back at him. Representatives from Ireland and Japan, India and Poland, the United States and Burkina Faso, Macedonia and the Bahamas all fixated on the former spiritual leader of the Irish and husband of the only known descendent of Takeo Nobunaga. Well, one of the two known descendants of Takeo Nobunaga. The other being his son, Ishiro'shea, who now resided on the planet Kelt running the universe's most famed drinking establishment, Cyborg Joe's Grill N' Go & The Why Not Saloon. But Father Flaherty wasn't thinking about his son, his wife, or the iconic martinis at Joe's; he was firmly focused on making sure that these officials didn't do anything stupid.

The Father cleared his throat. "Esteemed leaders of this

new Earth Alliance, I thank you for your time. I am honored to be here at this initial Global Summit of Joint Protection and Togetherness. I am Father Flaherty of New Tokyo, Ireland, and I come to you this day to discuss the impending invasion by the unknown military force that hovers above our planet."

The Father paused. He looked around the room to gauge the response. Nothing. *Someone, blink an eye, for God's sake. Oh, sorry, God.* His eyes caught those of his wife, Yumi. They lingered until she tossed back a swift smile. He took a deep breath.

"The last two solar cycles have been the most critical in our planet's history. After the Great LePaco War, we've started to rebuild. We've started to understand that it is up to us, our generation, at this very time in our existence, to halt the vicious cycle of war and violence that has plagued our planet for millennia. The great reimagining of a peaceful Earth could not have been done without the aid of our new friends from across the cosmos. I extend heart-felt thank-yous to the representatives here in attendance from the Bounty Hunters Union and the Gang of the Mystic Sabre; the security that you provided as we transitioned to this new, better Earth was paramount in our quest for improvement. To the ambassadors from Ootrel and To-To Megro Minor, your help in the literal rebuilding of our structures is something for which we will always be in your debt; to the ambassadors from Oscavia and Glyptodia, our appreciation for your assistance in getting the once unrivaled industrial might of our planet back on track could never be overstated. Our dear friends from Gartosh, how can we properly thank you? You were our voice to the rest of the universe; you told them our story and our drive to become something other than the haven of hate and violence that became our reputation. Lastly, and most importantly, to the last three remaining members of the Yehaso civilization—Venksplin, Sattlamora, and Lantejira—your third-party mediation allowed us to renew and revitalize long-forgotten partnerships and bonds between the great nations of Earth. You made us break bread instead of bones and have been one of the most crucial parts of this evolution. I'm not sure how you came to us, or why, but I do thank God that you did."

Father Flaherty paused again. The majority of the room applauded. The noted ambassadors shook hands and exchanged nods and smiles with the Earth leaders in attendance. The three beings from Yehaso stood at the side of the room, stoic in nature. The Father gestured in their direction and the applause escalated. The Yehaso smiled, all in unison, as if they shared the same mouth.

"However, our climb up this steep hill has encountered another peril, one that could potentially send us tumbling back to the ground and make all our progress for naught. That disease is the force above our fair planet. It grows by the day. More and more of LePaco's former cronies and yes-men arrive with more bombs, more lasers, more death and destruction."

Many in the audience squirmed uncomfortably. But their eyes remained fixated on the Father.

"I implore you in our hour of need that we lower our shields of distrust and allow our friends, the Yehaso, to lead our strategic initiatives in this battle."

He took in a deep breath and braced for impact. It came. Nearly every representative in attendance rose to their feet and began screaming in the Father's direction. With so many comments streaming at once, it came across as one large wordless howl. Yumi ran to the side of her husband and gripped his arm.

"Thank you," the Father whispered to his wife amidst the chaos.

The security at the event—primarily Gartoshian—settled down the riled up mob and restored some semblance of order.

The representative from Denmark rose to his feet and shouted, "Why should we give military control to these aliens? Is there not a skilled enough Earther for the job?"

The ambassador from Canada rose to her feet as the last word from the Dane faded. "And why should we trust these Yehaso? We barely know them. Sure, they can mediate—but that hardly qualifies you to be a general."

Lastly, the Portuguese official stood and, in a more measured voice, asked, "Weren't the Yehaso defeated by LePaco? That's why there are only three, right? Is that what we want? Our planet reduced to only a few survivors?"

With that question, the entire delegation became silent. Their focus was once again on the former spiritual leader of the Irish. But before the Father could say a word, his wife, Yumi Nobunaga-Flaherty, stepped in front of him and assumed the speaker position.

"My husband is a diplomat. He is too fair, too courteous for his own good. He is also a terrible salesman. Here's the truth. Honorable Jepsen of Denmark, the answer is no. There is not an Earthling that can handle this. Show me the last Earth general that led or participated in a battle off-planet. We've been too busy killing each other; we are out of practice in killing space invaders. Official Mulroney-Smithe of Canada, we are not asking them to be generals in our military. I doubt they would want that. They offered to provide us strategic concepts that can help prevent our planet from being overrun. That is all. It would be folly to refuse."

The Father peered out over the seated diplomats. Many

were frozen, wide-eyed with mouths agape. Others merely looked down at the floor.

My wife is a lot better at this than me, concluded the Father.

"And you, Mr. Lomba of Portugal, I believe we will be reduced to a few survivors if we *ignore* the Yehaso. This is not the time to start refusing outside help. As far as their history—" Yumi stopped abruptly.

The three Yehaso were onstage.

How'd they get up there without anyone noticing? the Father asked himself.

The Yehaso were humanoid in nature, roughly the same size as most Earthlings. All three members possessed bright white skin, as if they were made of bleached milk covered in fresh fallen show. They each had eyes of dazzling cobalt. Venksplin, the shortest of the three beings, made his way to Yumi. He bowed slightly. Yumi stepped aside and the alien stood front and center at the podium, facing the firing squad of Earth diplomats.

They all began to scream and shout in unison again, similar to the barrage that overwhelmed the Father. Venksplin stood motionless, without even a solitary blink.

Do they blink? thought the Father.

The Yehaso stroked his beard—the hair follicles were so straight and dense that it looked as if a solid block of blue ice extended from his ears beyond his chin—as the representatives continued to hurl questions and insults alike at the alien. Minutes passed and slowly, one by one, the diplomats began to sit and cease their questions.

"Thank you for the questions," Venksplin began in a pleasant, melodious tone. "I won't be able to answer them all today, and for that, I am truly sorry. However, I do want to address one concern that you have regarding the aid that we volunteered. We were not defeated nor driven out by

Admiral LePaco during the Great LePaco War." The crowd began to murmur, side conversations and under-the-breath comments escalated. "In fact, our home world drove away the advancing Four I's forces with considerable ease. Even at the height of our existence, the Yehaso were few in number. Populations smaller than some of your beautiful and noble cities such as Istanbul or Nice or Des Moines."

"Then what destroyed your planet? What reduced the Yehaso to you three?" asked Mr. Lomba.

"About the time that we drove the forces away, a great plague reached our planet. My colleagues—the caring and beautiful Sattlamora and the mighty and powerful Lantejira —and I had to witness our home be run over by..."

"Yes?" interjected Lomba. "What?"

"Run over by three titanic beasts," continued Venksplin. "Three world-destroying monsters from the depths of uncharted space. They feasted on our planet's soul. Killed everything and everyone in their path. And for reasons that we still are unsure of, they did not leave. We had to flee."

Not a single word left the lips of those in the audience. The Father stepped to the platform quickly.

"Leaders, colleagues, nations, as I stated earlier, I beg of you to let the Yehaso assist us in thwarting this attack," he began. "They have experience in defeating the Four I's— when the I's were a more unified force with more firepower, even. Let them help us. Thank you." The Father bowed to the attendees and stepped back.

The Honorable Valdemar Jepsen of Denmark stood up in the middle of the sea of seated officials. He tentatively raised his hand as if he needed permission to speak. His eyes squinted, then returned to their full size. His mouth opened and closed a handful of times as if he was going to say something but thought better of it. He did finally speak.

"Did you say monsters?"

CHAPTER 6

A WELL-MADE MARTINI

"**F**IRST TIME TO CYBORG JOE'S?" asked the bounty hunter.

Blop, the Blop from Blop stared back at Duke, his eyes unblinking, as if he didn't understand the question. Or was waiting on the Nova Texan to complete it.

"For your specific incarnation. *This* physical manifestation of Blop," Duke clarified.

"Ah, yes. It is," Blop answered, rather jovially...for a Blop. "And we...I...am very excited. This place has a certain reputation, even amongst the Blop."

"Well, here it is. Welcome," Duke proclaimed as he swung open the door, revealing the cavernous bar-gastropub-entertainment venue that was Cyborg Joe's Grill N' Go & The Why Not Saloon. Duke's eyes scanned the premises. It was almost exactly as it was before; maybe a little cleaner, but it was just like he remembered it. A smile crept over Duke's face. His gaze darted to the corner and his grin diminished quickly. The aged wall near the restrooms, battered and beaten over time, was repaired. The divots and burns and laser blast markings were patched up and painted over. Duke's thoughts lingered.

"It's a very nice wall," Blop added.

"Oh, yes, I'm sure it is," Duke replied, half-heartedly. "You know, Blop, that's where the portals were, the crown jewel of Cyborg Joe's. I must've forgot, for a split second, they were gone. It's still a little odd, ya know. Those portals *were* Joe's."

"I see," Blop stated. "The photographs and holograms that adorn its facade now are very appealing to the eye; an intelligent decorative enhancement, if that provides any consolation."

"Enough reminiscing," the bounty hunter said, snapping out of his trance. "We are at the best, well, at least the loudest bar in the galaxy; let's get us a drink. You have to try the martinis."

"Sounds exhilarating," Blop replied.

As the bounty hunter and the gooey alien made their way to the bar, they were greeted with handshakes, pats on the back, and any number of congratulatory remarks. At least, Duke was. Most in the bar seemed to be perplexed by Blop. They weren't a common species and, despite gaining some notoriety for their efforts at the Tournament of the Shield of the Colossal Calamari and the Great LePaco War, the majority of the universe's population had never seen a Blop from Blop. Regardless, Blop seemed to enjoy the attention, even if it was simply basic curiosity. Duke hopped up on a squeaky barstool and spun around. Less gracefully, Blop did the same. Immediately, Duke's smile returned.

"Mr. LaGrange, a pleasure as always. I think we were closing in on a record number of days without your patronage. In fact, I think we may have set it. I will have to consult the record book. The seventh edition comes out later this cycle," bellowed a hulking Glyptodian bartender.

"Earl, you giant hairy bastard, it's good to see you!" exclaimed Duke. He lunged over the bar top and grabbed the Glyptodian in a bear hug. "I missed you. How about you get us two martinis?"

As was customary with any native son or daughter of Glytopida, Earl was an exceptional purveyor of hospitality. Alcohol production and dissemination were such ingrained traits in the DNA of nearly all Glyptodians, they were birthrights. And Earl was the best at them. He was as synonymous with Cyborg Joe's as the Queen or the portals or the martinis.

"Coming right up, Mr. LaGrange. And you, sir. If I remember correctly, you are Blop." Earl gestured to the diminutive being next to Duke.

"Yes, why thank you," Blop replied with a slight nod of his head. "Impressive, my Glyptodian friend."

"Mr. LaGrange has recounted stories of bravery or valor featuring your kind on numerous occasions. It is an honor to have you at Cyborg Joe's. These drinks are on the house." Earl returned the bow.

Blop pivoted to face Duke.

"I like this place."

"I thought you would," Duke chuckled. "Most do. But they end up liking it too much."

"Case in point," blurted out a voice from behind the two. "Why this moron would choose that primitive rock of Neprius over the wonders of Joe's is beyond me."

"Po'l!" Duke vaulted from the barstool and engulfed the former Neprian freedom fighter in an embrace that matched the one he gave Earl moments prior. "I'm glad to see that you're still alive. I just assumed you would've done something stupid and got yourself killed, by now. I mean, since I'm not around to save your sorry ass."

"Funny, you jerk. Without you around, Ish has been able to actually book some competent musical acts. No fear of you starting melees and shooting up the place," Po'l replied.

"How'd you know about that little dustup with the Trampling Death Robots?"

"I'm pretty sure everyone knows that story. I think *you've* told me a dozen times. If you forgot, some local artist memorialized it in one of the restroom stalls."

"I'm both honored and disgusted. But it's good to hear, regardless. And, in all seriousness, it's good to see you again. I've been curious, actually both Ja'a and I have been curious...are you and Lutra...you know," Duke asked, smirking. "A thing?"

"It's complicated," Po'l answered, his eyes drifting downward.

"Sounds intriguing," Blop responded. "I'd love to hear more."

Duke tapped Blop on the shoulder, leaned over and whispered.

"Oh, sorry, friend Po'l, I've been informed that you gave off clues indicating that you do *not* wish to speak of your relationship with this Lutra," Blop began. "My ability to read subtle context clues and body language is somewhat limited as my species interactions with other life-forms is relatively new."

"No harm," Po'l responded, shaking his head dismissively. "But, Duke, why are you here?"

"And, more importantly, *how'd* you get here?" added yet another voice. *Lilly.*

The massive anthropomorphic musk ox from the third moon of Gartosh approached the trio. Duke leapt up but Lilly extended an arm, ceasing the bounty hunter's advancement.

"No LaGrange hugs for me right now, Duke. I have a

date and I don't want you messing up my fur. This took a long time," Lilly explained.

"You look marvelous, Lilly. Your date is quite lucky."

The musk ox blushed.

"Oh, and this is..."

"Blop, the Blop from Blop, I presume," Lilly interjected, finishing Duke's thought. "It's an honor. The other Blops have been such great allies to us and to all sentient beings."

Though the Blop didn't blush—as it probably was biologically unable to do so—he did extend his hand. The musk ox shook it.

"Thank you. This is my first ever handshake," Blop said. "I think I like it."

"I'm honored," Lilly replied, "but I'm not going to let Duke out of the question. How'd you get here? I thought you were trapped on Neprius."

"First off, 'trapped' isn't the right word. It was a choice to go there. Start over. With Ja'a. And, second, well...second..."

"I helped him get here," Blop interrupted. "My means are proprietary, of course. But we Blop aren't confined to some of the physical restrictions of most other beings in this universe so we just sort of 'jumped' here."

"That's the 'how,' sort of. What's the 'why'?" asked Po'l.

Earl returned and gently placed two martinis down in front of Duke and Blop. "I'm very curious, as well," added Earl.

Duke took a deep sip. He could feel the chilled liquid slide down his throat and into his belly. It was cool and comforting. The martini was a time machine, each taste bud that was coated in the luxurious elixir setting off a thousand memories at once. He closed his eyes and inhaled deeply, trying to catch the fleeting thoughts.

"We have a problem. A big problem. On Earth."

"Earth? Isn't Earth just one big problem?" asked Po'l.

"Now it's a problem *with Mazilda Cloax*," added Duke.

Lilly, Po'l, and Earl did not move. They all seemed to be digesting the news.

From around the corner of the bar, donning a sparkling emerald *shinobi shozoku*, emerged Ishiro'shea. He wore his hood but the extension that covered his nose and mouth was open. All eyes fixated on the ninja and newly minted owner of Cyborg Joe's.

"One question," Ishiro'shea began. "When do we leave?"

CHAPTER 7

A SIMPLE PLAN

THE BRIDGE OF THE *STARSPLITTER* was fairly quiet. For the most part, it seemed that her people were doing their jobs. Then again, Mazilda Cloax was much more comfortable crouching in dark, shadowy places readying herself to assassinate a political leader with one of her famed throwing daggers than on the bridge of a first-class starship about to go into a pitched battle. She hoped what looked right from the crew was actually right. If things got a bit hairy, she could always consult Az. The cyborg was tough and grizzled but, despite being a mercenary without a single personal allegiance not bound by monetary transaction, she trusted him. If you lived for money, you needed to be alive to collect. He was a survivor, accomplished in space battle, and hated bounty hunters; three traits that made her a bit more at ease with the current situation.

As she looked at the forward view screen, there it was. Earth. *How can that little ball of water cause so many problems?* she thought.

"Captain, Captain!" shouted Redd Warwick frantically as he sprinted across the bridge. He came to an abrupt halt an arm's length from Mazilda. Sweat trickled down his forehead. His eyes were red and wet. "Urgent news. Not good, Captain, not good at all."

"What is it, Redd?" Mazilda asked calmly.

"Our scout ship," he continued. "The one that you sent out earlier."

"Yes?"

"It's gone. I mean, it was detected by the Earth forces."

"And?"

"And it was blown to bits."

Mazilda could sense the heads of a few of the bridge officers and technicians nearby turning to try and listen in more intently. She placed her hand on Warwick's back—causing him to blush and avert his gaze to the ground—and she slowly guided him to a corner of the bridge out of earshot of the crew. Az followed them, a pace or two behind, so he could not only hear but so he could also keep tabs on the rest of the room.

"Calm down, Redd. So what happened?" Mazilda asked. "Details, please."

"No details. It was patrolling the sector that you mentioned. Seemingly following orders correctly. And boom. One of their defense systems was triggered and destroyed it in the blink of an eye."

"Did we get any useful intelligence?"

"No, Captain. But we lost—"

"Yes, yes. It's a shame but they had a mission, a job, and it seems that they failed," she interjected.

Redd's eyes were frozen, his mouth open. It was clear that he wasn't ready for her frigid demeanor. *And he was in a leadership position? Maybe LePaco wasn't flawless,* she thought.

"What should we do? Ready another scout ship, Captain?" he asked.

"No, that's not necessary. Rozz has devised a plan,

apparently, and it sounds like the potential intel from the scout ship wasn't critical to its success. Be ready for when I call you to the war room to discuss. Only senior leaders are to be notified. You, me, Az, Rozz, and Darfol-Chell. That's it. Got it?"

Redd smiled, saluted, and exited the bridge.

Before Mazilda could turn back around, she could sense Az's stare burrowing into her back.

"You have something to say?" she asked.

Az chuckled. "You don't seem too upset by the news of the scout ship's failed mission."

"People die. That's what happens in war," she retorted as she turned to face the death-dealing cyborg. "I'm surprised you didn't know that. Maybe your reputation is a bit overstated."

"Not that the scout ship was blown up. But that the intelligence was never gathered. I thought you would care more," Az replied.

Mazilda simply shrugged her shoulders. "Let's just hope that Rozz's plan works."

The *Starsplitter* was an impressive craft, no doubt about it, but the war room did not match the elegance and sophistication of the rest of the ship. It was more of a converted janitor's closet, with barely enough room to squeeze in a circular table. It was a tight fit for Mazilda, Az, Redd, and Darfol-Chell. It was an extremely tight fit for the large-gutted Tardasian.

"You sure we couldn't have this conversation in your quarters?" complained Rozz.

"You sure you couldn't try to lose some weight?" replied Az.

Rozz ignored the comment and placed a metallic cube on the table. In his hand was a remote; he keyed in a few codes and the holographic image hovered over the cube. It was Earth. His fingers continued to peck away at the remote; with each tap, a new image appeared or was high-lighted on the three-dimensional projection of the dangerous blue planet.

"Here's what we can decipher from our long-range scanners," he began. "Major military outposts, here and here. We want to avoid a direct invasion at those junctures."

"Makes sense," interjected Warwick.

Rozz immediately paused the delicate dance of his digits and glared at the officer. Darfol-Chell shook both heads in unison.

"Continue, please," Mazilda requested.

"As I was saying," Rozz continued, "there's no point in an attack there because, even if we win, the casualties will be enormous. Now this is a hypothesis that could have been confirmed with the intel from the scout but I still think it's fairly accurate: I think their terrestrial scanners have been impacted greatly by the cycles and cycles of the Gang Wars, as they call them. They are much fewer in number than a planet of their level of development and their scanning capabilities are moderate, at best. They likely won't be able to detect us even at the distance of their boring, lifeless moon. Unless they knew we were there."

"So, I'm assuming that's part of the plan?" Mazilda asked.

"Yes. It's fairly simple but it's foolproof. We send a sizable portion of our fleet behind their moon. We advance directly from our position now. Slow enough for them to command a large majority of their fleet at us. We start to engage."

"Our limited force versus the brunt of their crazed military?" asked Redd.

"Yes," Rozz replied, rolling his eyes. "I have another hypothesis. I also think that Earth's forces are much more worn down than most think. And fragmented. They've needed help rebuilding, it leads me to believe that they are hurting. From what I can tell, the Gartoshians and the other allies with any sort of military might have all vamoosed."

"Not to mention that they haven't had a focused space battle in countless cycles, outside of a few of their ships helping out on Kelt during the LePaco War. Their military industrial efforts have concentrated on localized combat," added Darfol-Chell.

"But we can't underestimate them," Mazilda replied. "Earthers aren't to be taken lightly, even if we have an airtight plan."

"Yes, the plan. As I was saying, we engage—whether it looks hopeless or not—and at the right time, our hidden moon force swoops in and cuts them off. We envelop them and crush them from all sides. The planet will be there for our taking. What do you think, Captain?"

"Simple. Easy. But it could work," she answered.

"Too easy?" inquired Az. Rozz shot him a nasty glance; when Az noticed it, the Tardasian cowered. "It does rely on the key assumption that they won't pick up on half of our force moving behind their moon. Are we worried they won't notice that our force was cut in half, mysteriously?"

"The ships in the rear of our fleet—stationed there strategically by myself—have not been scanned. They've been monitoring that particular act since I gave them the order upon arrival," Rozz replied smugly.

"Impressive, indeed," Az replied with a slight bow of approval.

Mazilda noticed Rozz's smugness growing.

"Okay, I think we're set. This should be easy to execute," Mazilda concluded.

"What about the mysterious alien allies?" added Redd.

"What?" asked the Darfol head of the Jungafallowian officer. "What allies?"

Mazilda looked at Az. He shook his head in confusion. She then glanced at Rozz. He was equally confused.

"The word is spreading on the ship. Everyone is talking about it. Earth has been rebuilding rapidly with the help of this unknown group of magicians or warriors or something. They have special powers and are military geniuses. Maybe the greatest in the universe. Apparently, with only a few thousand people, they destroyed an entire Armada Titan and a fleet of LePaco's top ships during the war."

"Greatest in the universe?" Rozz snarked. "Not possible. How come I've never heard of them?"

"We don't have time for fairy tales and legends," began Mazilda sternly. "We go on facts—and, at times, really strongly supported assumptions. Right, Rozz? Tell the crew members that these alien allies were made up; a pathetic, last ditch effort by the Earthers to gain a psychological advantage. You end that talk now, Redd. That's an order."

"Yes," Redd replied with a salute.

"Should I call it in?" Rozz asked.

"Please. Make sure everyone is ready to go by tomorrow. Get those forces behind that moon as soon as you're able. I'll be in my quarters," ordered Mazilda.

"Should I join you?" asked Az.

"No, I'm good. I have some things to sort out before battle."

"As you wish, Captain."

"Okay, Captain, the Earth force is within striking distance," shouted one of the tactical officers.

"Send in the hidden force! Now!" Mazilda commanded.

The Earth force was bearing down on Mazilda's fleet.

"I said tell them to go! Did you hear me, officer?" she screamed.

"I did, Captain. They aren't responding," he replied.

The bulbous Tardasian approached the officer and pushed him out of his chair. He jabbed away at the control panel.

"Listen here, you idiots. Go! Go! Go! This is the official signal. Attack!" he raged. "Now. Or you'll ruin everything!"

Only static permeated the communication channel.

"Scan their position," ordered Mazilda.

"Yes, Captain," replied Rozz. After some prodding at the controls, a grave expression took over his face.

"Rozz? What are you picking up?" inquired Mazilda. "Are you reading any ships?"

"Yes, Captain," he responded.

"Good, establish a connection and send them in now. We are about to be overwhelmed by the Earthers."

"No, not good, Captain," he continued, almost robotically. "Not our ships. Their ships."

"What? Where are *our* ships?" interjected Az. "What happened?"

"Gone. Destroyed," Rozz replied, emotionless.

Mazilda Cloax calmly rose from her seat and took in a deep breath. "Get us out of this mess. Full retreat. And fast."

CHAPTER 8

THE FATHER'S NEXT SPEECH

T HE FATHER'S WALK TO THE podium was a bit easier this time. The cheers and applause had already started. He would get to soak in the feeling of victory, the feeling of being right. More importantly, the feeling of his trust in beings paying off. The Father was a spiritual man, a spiritual leader, in fact, so he knew it wasn't proper for him to take so much joy in being proven correct—but he let himself enjoy the moment. Between the Gang Wars, fleeing in exile, and the conflict with Admiral LePaco, he felt he deserved this.

He positioned himself behind the podium, shoulders square, and peered out into the audience. It was the same cast of characters as it was days before—ambassadors, representatives, and attachés spanning nearly all of the nations of Earth—but, instead of the blank stares or expressions of those that were ready to pounce, it was a sea of smiles and wide-eyed admiration.

"Greetings again, esteemed leaders of the new Earth Alliance," he began. Immediately, he was interrupted by a burst of congratulatory cheers. He motioned for them to remain silent, but they continued; they all rose to their feet and applauded. He turned to his side and locked eyes with his wife; he blew her a kiss. "Thank you, thank you. It is truly a great day for Earth. And, of course, the real heroes are our friends, the Yehaso." The Father motioned to the three stoic beings standing directly behind him. "Before I turn the podium over to Venksplin, I also want to thank my wife, Yumi. As you know, she is the rock of our partnership. And the brains. And the beauty. And really everything. She pushed just as hard, if not harder than me, to make sure these wonderful allies had a chance to aid us in our efforts against Mazilda Cloax."

The cheers escalated again. Yumi bowed to the audience. The Yehaso managed a fragmented bow. It was clear that they were trying to mimic the Earth custom; it was equally clear that they weren't familiar with bowing. They all smiled, impeccably in synch, as the loudest ovation rushed through the room.

"Those in attendance and the great people of Earth watching this broadcast, I present to you the new heroes of Earth, the last remaining members of the Yehaso— Venksplin, Sattlamora, and Lantejira."

The Father stepped away from the podium and the pale-skinned Venksplin replaced him. Lantejira and Sattlamora followed a step behind and positioned themselves behind each of the smaller being's shoulders.

"It is great to be back in front of you all knowing that we were victorious in our mission," he began. He paused and smiled yet again as the applause escalated. Lantejira and Sattlamora, in yet another uncanny display of synchronization, smiled as well. "Please, ask us any questions that you may have. We Yehaso value trust and transparency above all."

It was Rafael Lomba of Portugal, a tall, slender man around fifty Earth cycles of age, that rose to his feet first and addressed the Yehaso. If anyone in the room *looked* like a diplomat, it was Mr. Lomba.

"Firstly, it is an honor to speak to you. We are in your debt," he started. The Yehaso all bowed, as rigidly as their first attempt. "I know this may come across as an inarticulate query, or at the very least, too broad to be considered appropriate, but how did you do it?"

"We give full credit to our past experience. It was not skill or anything that could be taught, but the simple recognition of a similar strategy employed by forces of Admiral LePaco on our planet," Venksplin began to explain.

Without warning and without any interruption to the cadence and flow of the reply, Venksplin stepped back into the spot behind his right shoulder, occupied by Lantejira. He in turn shifted to his left and stood where Sattlamora was previously. The slender female Yehaso was now in front, behind the podium. She was an eyelash taller than Venksplin but sported the same bleach-white skin—albeit with slightly more delicate features. Her eyes were an even more electric cobalt than her compatriots, dazzling under the concentrated illumination of the press.

"When LePaco attempted to invade our home world," she began in an equally melodic tone as Venksplin, "he hid the majority of his forces behind one of our eight moons, hoping to lure us out by showing us a much smaller, more manageable attack fleet. His sleight of hand was not successful on our people due to monitoring stations that we had placed on all of our satellite moons and nearby planetoids. You may think that we were paranoid, but invasions were a primary concern to the Yehaso, despite not being a regular occurrence. As your defense force began to assemble, we were fixated on the moderate size of the invading fleet. To try and achieve conquering a planet with the hearty reputation of Earth, most semi-intelligent beings would realize that you need a much more imposing military. It did not, as you would say, 'feel' right. So, the logical next step was simple: adjust your long-range sensors and scanners to monitor the backside of your moon and other nearby planets. Our prognostication proved successful."

The trio shifted again, this time the wide-shouldered Lantejira was now standing front and center. He was taller and broader than Venksplin and Sattlamora; his hardened ice-like beard did not extend as far as Venksplin's but it did have a more artistic design to it. What would have been viewed as sideburns on Earth stretched a full forearm's length from Lantejira's face, creating a sort of protective shield for his ears. Unlike the other two, blue tribal drawings zigged and zagged across his face.

"Once the scanners picked up on what we had anticipated, the next obstacle was to move the force behind the moon without being noticed by the opposing force. We needed the element of surprise since we weren't positive on the size of the armada stationed behind the moon," he stated in a deeper, more bellowing voice than his comrades. "That's when we made the call to our allies from the Bounty Hunters Union and the Mystic Sabre that had recently left. Both relished the opportunity to turn around and surprise the Four I's forces. They overwhelmed them in seconds and the Earth forces that were at the ready swooped in to finish the mission. The Union and Mystic Sabre were already heading back home before the rest of the enemy's fleet had any idea what had happened."

The Yehaso rotated again, bringing Venksplin back to the forward position.

"Any questions?" he asked.

The crowd was unusually silent. The officials looked around at each other, but no one stood, no one raised their hand, and—most shockingly—no one said a word.

The Yehaso were thorough but I've never seen anyone or anything shut up a room of self-righteous diplomats, thought the Father.

"Thank you," concluded Venksplin. All three Yehaso smiled in harmony and bowed.

"Oh wait," shouted Official Mulroney-Smithe of Canada. "Oh, sorry for yelling," she quickly apologized. "But we did have one question for the Yehaso. Something they said last time but never gave us an answer on. What are these monsters, these beasts, that you spoke of?"

Father Flaherty stepped in front of Venksplin.

"Like I said before, Official Mulroney-Smithe," began the Father, "details regarding the Yehaso's origins are not a topic of discussion for this press conference. Feel free to engage with them afterwards. If that's all, we will cut transmission. Thank you, everyone."

The broadcast ended.

"BLOP GOT ME FROM AN uncharted spatial pocket to Kelt in a literal blink of an eye, but the gummy bastard made us take the D.I.P.S. station to Earth," complained Duke. "And he made us pay for it."

"You survived," Lilly replied.

"Once you travel Blop, it's hard to go back to this," retorted Duke.

The *Deus Ex Machina* rumbled to a near stop and began to descend onto a rooftop landing pad in New Tokyo. The jungle of twisted metal, half-intact structures, and intensely fortified retaining walls looked much different now. The walls were gone and much of the debris had been removed. Trash didn't fill the streets—it had been replaced by a few well-manicured bits of shrubbery. *Is that a garden?* Duke asked himself. An area that cried despair and cruelty and savagery was now much more inviting, almost hopeful.

"Are you sure this is New Tokyo?" asked Duke.

Ishiro'shea replied with a thumbs-up.

Good to see that gesture again, thought Duke. "Well then kudos to your folks, Ish. I can't believe this urban dumpster is somewhat presentable. And in a damn short time."

"It looks lovely," added Lilly.

Po'l said nothing. His face was glued to the forward screen. Earth and New Tokyo, Ireland, in particular, were probably the farthest a place could get from Neprius. Even this new cleaner, more approachable version. Sure, Kelt had its areas that came with a certain type of unique charm. But this...this was Earth. This was New Tokyo, the heart of the much discussed, studied, and cursed Gang Wars.

The ship landed with a pronounced thud and began to power down. From the view screen, Duke could make out a band of humanoids and one Gartoshian approaching the ship.

"Looks like your folks," Duke said to Ishiro'shea. "And one of your cousins, Lilly?"

"Not everyone on Gartosh is related, you ignorant ass," she snorted.

"I know, I know. It's a joke," Duke said, waving his hands in the air in submission. "I know the Gartoshians were instrumental in helping Earth get its act together."

The burly musk ox stood up and focused her gaze on the screen.

"Know him?" asked Duke. "Or her?"

Lilly shook her head. "Unbelievable," she snorted and went back to her seat. She sat down, arms crossed. "Unbelievable," she repeated.

"Old boyfriend?"

"No."

"Old girlfriend"

"No."

"Then who?"

"It's my cousin," she said dejectedly.

Duke's grin almost ripped his cheek muscles from his skull.

———

As they made their way from the ramp out of the *Deus* to the platform, one of the humanoids in the welcoming party started to sprint towards them. It wasn't a particularly fast sprint, and it was a tad erratic as if the being wasn't accustomed to running. Ishiro'shea pushed Duke aside and darted toward the figure. The ninja embraced his mother, picking her tiny frame off the ground. His father—*the* Father—followed shortly after. As Duke, Lilly, and Po'l caught up to Ishiro, the rest of the Earth representatives enveloped them. They were mostly armed guards, heavy assault rifles in tow. But there were also three non-Earthers. Their skin glowed white-hot while their facial expressions were lukewarm. Duke couldn't place the species, and he had seen a lot of beings in his travels.

Father Flaherty extended a hand to the Nova Texan. Duke shook it.

"It's good to see you again, Duke," the Father said, still holding his firm grip. "It's good to see you all." He and Yumi both bowed in tandem to Duke, Lilly, and Po'l.

"And you," Duke replied. "Though I wish it were under better circumstances."

"About that," the Father began. "We just scored a decisive victory over the Four I's forces. Nearly wiped them out."

"Huh. Well, that does explain the lack of enemy ships on our way in," responded the bounty hunter. *What was Blop talking about, then?* Duke asked himself.

"Yes, it was a rousing victory. It seems that you came all this way to join our victory party," Yumi added. "We have parades planned for nearly every major city on the planet over the coming weeks."

"I love a good party," chimed in Po'l.

"So, is Mazilda captured? Killed?" asked Duke.

"No, we didn't take any prisoners. We destroyed their fleet. I'm not sure if she survived and retreated or if she was one of the casualties," answered the Father.

"Impressive. Congrats, I guess," Duke mumbled.

"You don't seem too happy, Duke," said Yumi. "This is a great victory for us, especially since the people joined together as one unified Earth. Some thought the progress made after the LePaco War was a one-off aberration; this proves that we are a cohesive and progressive Earth now."

"No, no, please don't interpret my comments as anything other than happiness. I'm good...it's all good," responded Duke.

Ishiro'shea's parents bowed again.

"Before I forget, let me introduce you all to our newest allies, the Yehaso," the Father began, ushering the three icy-skinned beings to the forefront. "They might be the biggest reason for our defeat of the invading force."

"You don't say," replied Duke. He removed his hat and nodded his head. "Seems like you three deserve a huge thank-you and maybe a huge mug of Glyptodian Summer Ale. My name's Duke. Duke LaGrange. Adventurer. Trailblazer. Poet. A true man of the universe."

The Yehaso's faces did not budge.

Tough crowd, thought Duke.

"And this is my trusted comrade and owner of Cyborg Joe's, Ishiro'shea," he continued.

"That's our son," Yumi whispered to the Yehaso. They responded to her with a simple nod.

"And this is Lilly Arnaq, the pride of Gartoshian Moon Colony #3, and one of the toughest ladies in the cosmos.

She missed her date to come here. And finally, this is Po'l, of the distant planet Neprius. Don't let his dumb, primitive look fool you, he was an accomplished freedom fighter on his home world."

Po'l shoved Duke.

"I'm kidding," Duke replied. "He's a good dude...and not dumb."

The Father turned to the Yehaso. "Duke, Ishiro'shea, Lilly, and Po'l were instrumental in defeating Admiral LePaco and saving the universe," he explained. "Duke was the one who pulled the trigger."

"I see," the shortest Yehaso replied coldly.

Really tough crowd, thought Duke. *Saving the universe usually elicits a bigger response than that.*

Duke unsheathed Ol' Betsy from his Ootrelian leather holster that clung to his back. The security detail drew their firearms at this action, but the Yehaso remained frozen.

"This is it," explained Duke. "This is the instrument that took out that crazed maniac. Want to touch it?"

The Yehaso who had spoken did not blink. Nor did his two compatriots.

"How 'bout you, big guy?" Duke asked the muscular Yehaso. Nothing. He turned his attention to the female Yehaso. "Someone as beautiful and elegant as you has to understand the importance of such an artifact."

The Yehaso remained still as if they couldn't see or hear the bounty hunter.

"It killed LePaco, for crying out loud," Duke shouted in frustration.

"So, Duke and crew, let me introduce the Yehaso," the Father said, stepping between Duke and the three aliens. "This is Venksplin. Lantejira. And Sattlamora."

They all smiled simultaneously and bowed.

"Pleasure to meet you all," Venksplin spoke.

"We've enjoyed the tales that have been told regarding your exploits," added Sattlamora.

"Very high on entertainment value," concluded Lantejira.

"Tales?" Duke said, his brow furrowed. "Entertainment, you say?"

"Yes, very exciting stuff," Sattlamora added. "Yumi and the Father told us everything once we learned of your arrival."

"They did, did they?" Duke replied.

"I've never heard of the Yehaso," chimed in Lilly. She placed one of her massive hands on Duke's shoulder and moved him behind her. "Where is your planet? I'd love to learn more."

The Yehaso rotated their position and Sattlamora was about to speak before her voice was drowned out by the screams of a charging Earther. He was darting towards the group at an alarming pace. However, the voice was recognizable.

"Everyone! Everyone!" he shouted as he approached.

Yeop.

Ishiro's schoolmate slowed to a halt. His eyes locked on Duke, Ishiro'shea, Lilly, and then Po'l. He hesitated and then dove at them, grasping each in a friendly hug.

"I didn't know you guys were here," he said. He took a step back to look at them and put his hands on his hips. "Wow. This is awesome."

"Yeop," Yumi interrupted. "Why were you running out here so frantically?"

"Oh yeah," Yeop shook his head wildly as if he was trying to recover his initial train of thought. "The sensors just picked up something. Beyond the invaders' original position. I think they're regrouping. Maybe a counterattack?"

"I see," the Father said solemnly. He looked at his wife. "Go put a hold on any celebrations until we know what this is."

Yumi nodded in agreement, hugged her son one more time, and scurried back inside with three armed guards behind her.

"Everyone, let's go see if we can figure out what Mazilda or her cronies are up to," ordered the Father.

He motioned to the group to follow him. Duke sheathed Ol' Betsy and looked at his best friend and trusted sidekick.

"Maybe these cats aren't as good as they thought they were," he whispered.

Ishiro'shea simply rolled his eyes.

CHAPTER 10

A LIVELY DEBATE

T HE ROOM WAS PRETTY DAMN boring. Muted white walls. A few monitors scattered about. A big oak desk in the center. But in the span of a few minutes, it was packed. Despite this being a matter of planetary security, no one asked Duke, Ishiro'shea, Lilly, and Po'l to leave. They simply blended in—and that was saying something when your party includes an anthropomorphic musk ox from one of the moons of Gartosh. Duke couldn't ascertain if their presence was allowed because of their close connection to the Flahertys or because he was regarded as the savior of the universe for his heroic disposal of Admiral LePaco. He wanted to think it was the latter.

In the room and getting settled around the table were the Father, Yumi, the Yehaso, and a handful of military personnel. They all looked slightly different—definitely Earthers—but from the various nooks and crannies of the mixed-up planet. Despite what was likely cycles upon cycles of military experience, none of them spoke—they all stared at the Yehaso.

Wow, they are in charge, surmised Duke.

"What is it?" asked a dark-skinned female official. The

lights were substantially subdued in the room, but it was bright enough to ricochet off of the woman's medals and into Duke's eyes. "Is it Cloax?"

"I thought we destroyed her forces?" added a light-skinned, silver-haired attendee. He sat next to the woman but sported far fewer medals. "What's our current intel?"

"Yeop," began the Father, "can you share with the group everything that we know?"

Yeop bowed to the point in which his nose almost touched the floor. Then he pressed a button on a raised plat-form extending from the wall. The wall opened up to reveal a large screen. On the screen was a fairly crude layout with live data streaming from the remote sensors.

"We noticed this blip a few moments ago," he said, pointing to a cluster of pixelated dots behind what appeared to be the graphical representation of Mars. "At first, we made sure it wasn't simply a really spunky collection of asteroids between Mars and Jupiter. It wasn't. The readings were much different. We ran some more scans, and nothing was conclusive. But based on their exit trajectory, we believe it's three new closely-packed battalions coming back to make another attempt at invasion."

"The readings proved that out?" asked the heavily medaled female.

"No, not exactly. They aren't the typical signatures of a Jungafallowian ship or a Four I's ship, for that matter. But many of the craft in the recent skirmish had unique or partially cloaked signatures, so our best estimation is that these squadrons are made up of unregistered or heavily altered military vessels."

"They appear to be moving toward us at an alarming speed," added the official.

"Yes, these ships appear to be substantially more

advanced than the previous—both faster and larger," replied Yeop.

Nearly all of the military officials in the room, including the Flahertys, turned toward the three Yehaso.

"Thoughts?" the Father asked.

Venksplin shifted in his seat. Lantejira looked down at the ground. Sattlamora squinted her eyes. For the first time, Duke noticed their stoicism wasn't quite so, well, stoic.

Sattlamora spoke first. "I'm afraid that your projections are faulty."

"That's good," replied the silver-haired man, leaning back in his chair.

"I'm afraid not," countered Venksplin. "We are very aware of these unique signatures. And unfortunately, a second wave of attacks from the assassin Mazilda Cloax and her followers would be preferable to what is about to be here in our midst."

"And that is?" asked the less-medaled official.

It was Lantejira, the hulking Yehaso, who stood up and focused his gaze directly at the Father and Yumi. "These are the beasts that destroyed Yehaso."

No one replied. Everyone remained in their seat.

"Wait a second, space monsters?" blurted out Duke. All eyes quickly fixated on the bounty hunter.

"Who are you?" snapped a grizzled military leader from the far corner of the room. "How'd you get in here?"

"Um, you don't know me?" Duke began. "I'm Duke LaGrange. Adventurer. Trail—"

"Duke was the one who defeated Admiral LePaco; well, he's the one who killed him," interjected Yumi. "He was the one who worked directly with Queen Joe from Kelt in that final battle. He's our guest."

"Yes, Duke LaGrange, these are space monsters" answered Sattlamora in a slightly sweeter tone than her compatriots. "These are space monsters that have destroyed more worlds than we care to speak."

"How can we stop them?" asked the Father.

Venksplin stood. "You can't."

"What do you mean you can't? There's always a bigger weapon, a badder animal," shouted Duke.

"Perhaps," answered Sattlamora. "But we have not seen one or know of one's existence. These monsters ate our world."

The room fell silent. The eyes of the attendees danced from one official to the next, looking for answers. No one spoke. *Never thought I would be bummed that a Four I's invasion fleet led by Mazilda Cloax wasn't beelining towards me*, thought Duke. After a few moments, all gazes seemed to fixate on the Yehaso. They remained unfazed: no blinks, no shuffles, no sweat dripping from the brow.

"Okay," began Duke, "we aren't going to have a chance if we just sit here, awkwardly staring into one another's eyes."

"And what authority was given to you to address this council as if you were in charge?" asked the silver-haired military official in an agitated tone. "We agreed to let these three help us strategize but nothing about you and your lot."

"Calm down, Lieutenant. You seem a bit cranky. I have some sleeping serum back on my ship if you need a nap," Duke replied.

"Get this miscreant out of here," barked the official. "And I'm a colonel, son, not a lieutenant."

The Father stood and extended his arm in front of Duke. The bounty hunter remained still, his mouth closed.

"We did agree to let the Yehaso help us; and they saved us," exclaimed Yumi. "I think our track record speaks for itself. Duke should be allowed to participate freely. We will take responsibility for him and his crew."

"And I saved the gods damn universe," blurted Duke. "I think I have some experience in these situations."

The room erupted in a lively debate. Arguments regarding Duke and his crew's inclusion in the session, whether the monsters were indestructible, was this a big rouse by Mazilda, and more topics ranging from the practical to the extremely hypothetical—borderline fantastical— filled the space. The Yehaso remained as silent as ever, even when being addressed directly.

A loud crack rang out. The heavily fortified table in the center of the room was split in two. All discussions ceased immediately. Lilly stood there, her eyes inflamed a vivid crimson and her nostrils pulsing. She inhaled deeply.

"I think it's time that we all calm down and discuss how we're going to deal with these approaching planet maulers. I'm not saying that this is what we should do but what *I* would do is ask these wonderful new friends of ours everything they know about these beasts. Maybe we can think of a game plan to kill them...or capture them...or reroute them. We solve nothing by screaming about who should or shouldn't be in the room."

There seemed to be a silent agreement from all parties in the room. Heads started to turn to the three beings from Yehaso.

Venksplin spoke. "The three beasts are known to our people as the Cosmoses."

CHAPTER 11

THE COSMOSES

"OUR PLANET WAS NEVER AS populous as Earth," started Venksplin, all eyes fixated on the three unpigmented beings from Yehaso. "But we were a thriving civilization with industry, environmental consciousness, general peace. It had taken us thousands of cycles and much war and pain to reach our stage of enlightenment—but we did."

"The day was no different than any other," began Sattlamora, picking up the conversation from Venksplin as if they had been a single being. "If I recall, it was very bright. And warm. Our people were still rejoicing from our victory over Admiral LePaco and his army. Then the information began to reach us. It reached every last corner of Yehaso. We were being invaded."

"We had no known enemies at that time," Lantejira said, taking over the speaking duties. "We did not have many neighbors in our system—none that could travel through space or mount an invasion. The few that we did have, we had finalized treaties or trade partnerships many cycles earlier. We could not understand why some of our beautiful cities were being attacked."

"But they were," continued Venksplin. "Some from the sky. Some from the sea. Some from the very soil that our cities and towns and villages rested on. The three destructors were thought to be the Cosmoses. In one of our ancient religions, long abandoned, they were a trio of marauding evil spirits that came from the heavens and manifested themselves as horrific monsters. Some Yehaso actually believed this was the case. Regardless, the beasts provided no opportunity for escape and did not yield for a single moment until the whole of Yehaso was reduced to a lifeless rubble."

"But you three survived?" asked Po'l.

"Not just us three. Many more of us survived the initial attacks," answered Sattlamora. "The military outposts were hit first—these were creatures that knew what they were doing—but we had enough to put together a counteroffensive. We three were stationed together on the same striker ship. The counter was not a successful endeavor."

"When all hope seemed lost and our once majestic home was nothing but a burning pile of death and chaos below us, we fled. Luckily, our striker is a pretty durable deep space vehicle. I'm not sure how many Yehaso survived the failed counterattack. We have tried to establish contact, but it has been unsuccessful. We maintain hope that not all perished," concluded Lantejira.

There was a long silence. It was clear that those in the room were trying to process this story. Duke couldn't help but visualize the crazy blue planet of Earth up in flames at the hands of these cosmic beasts.

"They don't have the element of surprise this time," chimed in the heavily medaled military official.

"That is correct, General Munger," replied Venksplin with a courteous nod in the General's direction.

"So, can you tell us everything that you know about

these Cosmoses, militarily-speaking?" asked Yumi Nobunaga-Flaherty. "What assault techniques did you use that proved effective? Any hypotheses on what might be damaging to them?"

"During our escape and hiding, before we discovered Earth, we had compiled some ideas on how to defeat them. We have not tried any—they are all in the theoretical stage," Venksplin explained. "But we are hopeful. I see no reason, from a technological or application standpoint, that we can't employ them here with your resources."

Duke walked over, splitting the chairs in between the two most decorated military personnel, and hoisted himself up until his posterior was resting on the edge of the table. They both scowled. *I guess this isn't proper protocol.* He grinned at both of them.

"So why did these beasties pick the Yehaso to feast on?" asked the bounty hunter. "I'm sure there were some other tasty planets to gobble up. Or was it just bad luck?"

"Or even what they are? I mean what they *actually* are? They are just blips on our sensors right now," added the silver-haired military official.

"Of course, Colonel Tott," answered Sattlamora, facing the Colonel.

Are they ignoring me? thought Duke.

"The Cosmoses," Sattlamora continued, "were unknown to our people until the attacks—but they were all familiar."

"Great. Riddles," scoffed Duke in a hushed tone. He noticed the Yehaso female glance at him. *Ten points for perceptivity.*

"The Cosmoses are fixtures in the most ancient of our planet's religions. That doctrine and its worshippers died out millennia ago but the stories and images of the three Cosmoses survived in the form of stories that one would tell their offspring. They represented the end of times, the final destruction, the death of the Yehaso. They were the punch line to a lesson. Treat the planet well because a polluted planet will attract the Cosmoses. Be good in school because uneducated Yehaso are the Cosmoses' favorite snack. Be kind to your mother or she will call the Cosmoses to come and eat your friends. Along those lines."

Grim. Really grim, thought Duke.

"But they turned out to be real?" asked Colonel Tott. "What you thought were fixtures in a crazy, made-up religion turned out to be real?"

"We don't have to worry about that on Earth," snickered someone from the back. The Father quickly turned and stared into the collection of military officials, trying to isolate the culprit.

"Yes, Colonel," replied Venksplin. "Unfortunately, the old thinking proved correct. And somehow the Yehaso attracted the Cosmoses. We weren't sure if it was the skirmishes with LePaco—because we had wars in the past that did not produce the appearance of these space demons—or if it was simply the total eradication of belief in their existence. Either way, they showed up. And they destroyed our home."

"What are we dealing with here, Venksplin?" asked General Munger.

"Yeah, how big are these beasts?" added Tott.

It was Lantejira that spoke. "There are three. Three giants. Three titans. The smallest being able to tower over your largest human-made structure. And destroy it with a single step. They are of three different origins—all unknown."

"Hell of a description," interjected Duke. "You got any specifics?"

Lantejira continued. "The First Cosmos attacks from

the sky. In the old religion, it is referred to as the Winged Death. The Second Cosmos prefers the watery depths of the oceans. It is called the Aqua Demon. The Third Cosmos is the Underlord and—"

"Let me guess, it comes from *under* the ground," interrupted Duke. "But since they are all flying through space to get here then we can assume that they can all fly to some degree, right?"

"Duke, calm down," Yumi whispered to the bounty hunter, gripping his forearm. "Let them speak."

For a second, Duke felt embarrassed for his outburst. But it was only a second.

A collective gasp filled the room. All heads pivoted towards the view screens.

"How'd they get here so fast?" shouted Colonel Tott.

"The Cosmoses' ability to traverse space seems to be beyond anything we could have thought," Venksplin replied. "We didn't know."

"They're faster than any technology that we've ever seen," added Lilly. "This is amazing."

"The concept and constraints of physical travel seem to be meaningless to them," added a stunned Sattlamora.

No biggie. I've seen Blop do that too, Duke said to himself.

"Enough! We have a planet to defend," screamed General Munger. "Alert every branch of planetary defense. Let's get that perimeter up. Let's show them we mean business."

"Yes, General!" answered the uniformed personnel in the room.

"Colonel," Munger began, "get on the horn and let the Gartoshians know what's about to go down. I want someone in this universe to be made aware. Might as well call the Bounty Hunters Union and the Mystic Sabre. I don't expect any help after all they've done for us already, but you never know. You know what? Just tell anyone who will listen. If they get past us, who knows who'll be next."

The war room wasn't in total chaos, but the anxiety level had risen to at least a mild panic. Regardless, the soldiers seemed to be fulfilling the orders as they were being barked at them by General Munger and Colonel Tott. Duke strolled up to the monitor that captured the visuals of the three Cosmoses hurtling towards Earth.

"Now those are some ugly bastards," he said to himself.

A light tug was felt on his right shoulder. It was a hand. It was Venksplin's hand, specifically.

"Fellow space traveler," he began, "have you ever had to battle giant monsters?"

CHAPTER 12

THE WINGED DEATH

THE WAR ROOM WAS EMPTY outside of Duke, Ishiro'shea, Po'l, Lilly, Yumi Nobunaga-Flaherty, and a new table. The military personnel had scurried off to set up the defenses. The Father escorted the Yehaso to what, Duke assumed, was an even more secret and even more protected bunker. The Earth wasn't about to lose their alien guidance.

"How'd the evacuation go?" Duke asked Yumi as he joined the rest of the party at the freshly delivered table.

"Considering we have no idea as to where they're exactly going to land, I'd say pretty good. I'm just hoping we didn't move them from a safe zone to ground zero by mistake," she replied. "They got in range so quick. I just... just can't believe it."

"I've never seen anything like it," Lilly added. "I've never seen something biological move that fast in open space."

Ishiro'shea turned in his chair and stood up quickly. His chair rolled back and struck the edge of the table with ferocity. He glided over to the screens. In addition to the satellite feeds pulling in imagery outside of the Earth's atmosphere, there was a constantly rotating display of live camera footage from the cities that had been designated as potential targets for the Cosmoses. It shuffled the feed with every blink of the eye. On the back wall was a plethora of news broadcasts from across the globe; the impending attack had taken over the airwaves and served as a good method of disseminating emergency protocol to the millions of citizens who were likely to be in harm's way.

The ninja focused his attention on the rapidly rotating city views. His eyes remained fixated but he pointed to the largest screen, where the Cosmoses were being monitored.

"There's only two," exclaimed Po'l. "Where's the..."

"Winged Death?" finished Yumi.

Ishiro's glare remained steadfast. He then tapped the screen rapidly at a black dot hovering over a skyline. *This isn't good*, thought Duke. By the time Yumi noticed her son's signal, the view had passed.

"You know you can talk, right?" said Duke.

"Oh yeah," replied his emerald-clad compatriot. "Habit. And I don't think I really care for it, if I'm being honest."

Not good for someone who owns a bar, Duke thought.

The feed's rotation continued.

"It's about to appear...there!" shouted Ishiro'shea.

The black dot was much bigger now and it hovered over the skyline of a metropolitan spread. Duke could more accurately make out the appearance and size of the First Cosmos—the Winged Death. *This is bad, very bad*, he told himself.

"What city is that?" asked Duke.

Yumi squinted intently as the image quickly changed.

"It's in America. It appears to be over Chicago."

Lilly knelt down below the screens and opened up a small latch. She tapped in a few codes and the feed quickly shot back to the scene in question.

"That should do it. This should give us a stable view of the city," she explained.

"Do we want that?" asked Po'l.

"Better that we know what we're up against," replied Duke.

"We? What *we* are up against? Surely, you mean the legions of soldiers and war machines from Earth," the Neprian retorted.

"Sure. That's what I meant," the bounty hunter answered. "But it's good for us to assess. You never know when they might need our expert opinion on these matters. Remember, saving the universe is our thing."

There wasn't another mutter. All eyes slowly rotated back to what was unfolding above the Chicago skyline.

The Winged Death had arrived.

Chicago was a city that most non-Earthers knew. It had been the capital of Earth for hundreds of cycles during some of the bloodiest and most renowned wars. It didn't have the best reputation in the galaxy but, on the monitor, Duke thought it was quite beautiful. Compared to many of the planet's major metropolitan areas, Chicago had retained much of its ancient look. Timeless skyscrapers somehow remained intact for millennia as a reminder of the city's heritage as a captain of industry and innovation. The relics would have towered over any building in the whole of Nova Texas. If Nova Texas had mountains, these buildings would have towered over them too.

The satellite view feeding the monitor was of a considerable swath of real estate; the direct center of the screen squarely focused on a dense collection of concrete and glass structures. In the foreground, Duke made out a river that split the cluster of buildings and presumably led to a larger body of water.

Hovering above the cityscape was the First Cosmos. The Winged Death. It hurtled to the ground and landed with all four hooves on a street that ran parallel to the river. A tremor reverberated through the city, at least the parts that were visible on the monitor. Smoke and debris rose up from under the creature, silhouetting the unusual beast against the backdrop of the doomed city.

Duke had never seen anything even remotely resembling the Winged Death. He had heard stories of centaurs and Minotaurs and other similar "taurs" from his childhood; but he thought that was due to his culture's reliance on horses and cattle. It was natural to idolize or mythologize such critical elements to your planet's survival. But those creatures depicted in Nova Texan folklore shared only a passing similarity to the monster that flattened forty-story buildings like they were made of mashed potatoes. The Winged Death had the body of a horse, had the horse possessed a tail featuring three crystalline shards extending from its tip. The ruddy brown body transitioned into a lavender-skinned humanoid torso, muscular and pocked with scars and bruises. The Winged Death's arms branched out into four-fingered hands with nails as sharp as its tail spikes. Atop the massive torso was a monstrous head with a single eye and a single horn protruding from the forehead. As it wailed, it flashed a mouth of seemingly never-ending teeth.

As hideous and grotesque as the First Cosmos was, when it reared back on its hind quarters and stretched its wings—each as long as a city block—it would have been hard pressed to call it anything other than majestic. Then it reduced a museum to nothing but a pile of dust and pebbles...and it was an ugly destructive abomination again.

In the distance, there appeared to be a collection of shapeless blurs pooling together to form a bigger shapeless blur. The blur was heading toward the beast. As it came into focus, it was clear what was approaching the beast. Tanks.

"They're sending in the cavalry," said Duke.

"They're going to need a much bigger cavalry," replied Lilly.

CHAPTER 13

CHICAGO VERSUS THE SPACE MONSTER

[THE BROADCAST'S TITLE SCREEN DISSOLVES AND TRANSITIONS TO A DESK; BEHIND IT ARE A DARK-SKINNED EARTH FEMALE AND A SMALL ANDROID. THE SET IS BARREN, SPORTING NO LOGOS, CALL SIGNS, OR THE GRATUITOUS CITYSCAPE GREEN SCREEN BACKING.]

FEMALE ANCHOR: Hello, Chicago, this is Andrea Avalon from *Breakfast with Andrea and Holt*. We are coming to you today from a special remote bunker, well outside of the devastation that's impacting our great city. As you can see, Holt Stevens is not with me right now. He is actually on location near downtown and we will be going to him in a few to get live updates on this...uh, space monster... that's attacking our city.

ROBOT ANCHOR: [clears his throat]

ANDREA AVALON: And sitting in today for Holt is a special guest. Many of you know him as the voice of the final edition of the Tournament of the Shield of the Colossal Calamari on Psitakki. He's a veteran of over forty-two thousand broadcasts, including the likes of the Slinky

Racing Nationals to the Extreme Armadillo Juggling Grand Prix to Paint Drying Watching Battles on Gorma Gorma Zed. Yes, you know him, you love him...wait, I'm not reading that.

ROBOT ANCHOR: Read it, Andrea. *Beep.*

ANDREA AVALAON: I'm not reading that, it's beneath me.

ROBOT ANCHOR: It's in the contract, Andrea. *Beep.*

ANDREA AVALON: Fine. You know him, you love him, it's everyone's favorite spunky little android, Randy.

RANDY: Hello, Earthers! *Boop. Beep.* It's great to be on your funky little planet. Looks like I picked a good time. It's not often that you get to witness an extinction-level event in person. I'm excited! Are you, Andrea? *Boop.*

ANDREA AVALON: Are you insane, you weaselly little gearbox? My home is being leveled by some weird flying cyclops horse thing and you ask if I'm excited?

RANDY: Well, I'm excited. *Beep.* I've made a career of adding my commentary to the universe's most bizarre and fascinating spectacles. *Beep. Boop. Boop.* And this is a new one for yours truly. An enraged cosmic monster is pulverizing one of the most populated metropolitan areas on the planet; it makes the squabbles in the Tournament of the Shield look like a rousing game of pat-a-cake...if the participants are Bubble Wrapped and aren't actually allowed to touch each other. What do you think, Andrea? *Beep.* Do you think the city has a chance to stop this carnage? *Boop. Beep.* Or will this titan of terror win the day? *Boop.*

ANDREA AVALON: You disgust me. I'm out of here. I'm not going to be part of this garbage.

[Andrea Avalon throws a stack of papers at Randy and exits the set.]

RANDY: Is this a good time to ask you out?

[A minute of dead air. Screen goes black. The broadcast

returns and Randy is by himself at the desk, now positioned in the direct center. At the very right of the screen, there is a humanoid arm.]

RANDY: *Beep.* You're in the shot! Move! *Boop.*

[The arm disappears.]

RANDY: Damn makeup people. What type of operation are you running here? *Beep. Boop.*

VOICE FROM OFF CAMERA: You're on the air, Randy.

RANDY: *Boop.* Shit. *Boop.*

VOICE FROM OFF CAMERA: You can't say "shit" on the air.

RANDY: *Beep. Beep.* Well, I just did. *Beep.* And we're back, fight fans. Chicago versus the Space Monster. Beep. Unfortunately, our ravishing co-host, Andrea Avalon, had to leave. I'm sure she'll be back because who can resist Randy? Right? *Beep.* I'm getting word that some moron is down near the war zone. We'll send it to him, I guess. *Beep.* I'm taking two-to-one odds that he gets squashed within the first three minutes. *Beep.*

[Broadcast quickly jumps to a reporter with a microphone. The camera is zoomed in tight on his face. The city and the Winged Death are visible in the background.]

REPORTER: Chicagoans, this is Holt Stevens of *Breakfast with Andrea and Holt.* I don't have any words for what I'm witnessing today. Our city has seen a lot over its lifetime, there's no doubt, but I don't know if we've faced a force of nature of this magnitude. Maybe the only greater monster to our planet has been...ourselves.

[The camera zooms in on Holt Stevens' face. A single tear falls. The broadcast immediately returns to the studio set.]

RANDY: *Beep.* Are you kidding me? *Boop. Beep.* You are a stone's throw away from a colossal mega-beast ripping apart your city and you use this as your platform to take an overplayed swipe at your race? *Boop.* Hey buddy, if you can hear me, you don't need to worry about how dumb humans are right now, you need to worry about that one-eyed horse monster that just pushed over a skyscraper. *Beep.* Earthers are so weird. *Beep. Beep.*

[The broadcast returns to Holt Stevens on location.]

HOLT STEVENS: I'm having a hard time hearing the mothership. Is that you, Andrea? Hello. Okay, well it looks like we're still on the air. To bring you up to speed, this monster touched down a few minutes ago on ancient Wacker Drive, running alongside the river, and proceeded to topple most of the buildings on the riverfront with a few swift kicks from his horselike hind legs. Luckily, the emergency evacuations did manage to empty the city of much of its population, otherwise downtown Chicago would be less of a metaphorical graveyard and more of the literal kind.

[The camera pans to the creature.]

HOLT STEVENS: As you can see, this creature—the Winged Death is the name that's being leaked out by government officials—is cutting through the skyline of Chicago as if it was made of soggy crackers. What's he doing now? He appears to be readying for a leap. Yes, there he goes! He's now on the north side of the river. Oh no! No! Stop that! The Winged Death has both hands on our iconic, beloved Marina Towers. Those joining us from across the country and the world might know them better as the "corncob" buildings. They've remained a fixture of the Chicago riverfront for thousands of cycles, though uninhabited for most of that time. No! Don't do it! The beast has just ripped one tower from the ground like it was picking a weed. It's hoisting it over his head and...oh my god. It just threw the tower back over the river. Five more buildings are gone, just like that. Oh, the humanity. What have we done to deserve this? Not again, not again...the other Marina Tower has just been knocked into the river with a single clubbing blow from this horrid monstrosity.

[The camera returns to Holt Stevens with the monster in the background.]

HOLT STEVENS: I'm not sure we can stay much longer; I just received word that military aid is en route and should be here in moments. The Winged Death's rampage is something out of our own long dead mythology. The really bad ones where no one comes and saves the day. I'm just hoping that our forces can stop this brute. Right now, as you can see, it's focused its attack near the river but—oh, wait. It's taken to the air. Listen to that howl! Its scream alone is shattering glass across the city. If the ability to pound our largest buildings into dust with a single flick of your hand isn't enough, it has a banshee's scream that can seemingly pierce the sound barrier. What else can this grotesque space monster do? Let's hope that we've seen the worst it...you've got to be kidding! The Winged Death, while lingering over the city just let loose a blast, uh, a ray of some kind, from its eye. This thing can shoot lasers from its eye? We're all dead! Dead! It can fly and shoot lasers from its eye! Are you seeing this, people? Are you seeing this thing? I give up. We are witnessing the end of our city. The end of our planet.

[The broadcast returns to the studio set.]

RANDY: That's not good. *Beep.* That's all I got, folks. This doesn't look good. *Beep.* The creature's blast essentially leveled an entire section of the city. It's now entirely in flames. *Beep. Beep.* Good luck, Earth. I need to get my little android ass off this doomed rock! *Beep. Boop. Beep.*

[Randy exits the set. The camera remains fixated on the desk for a few moments. Then the broadcast goes black.]

CHAPTER 14

THE MILITARY VERSUS THE SPACE MONSTER

DUKE AND ISHIRO'SHEA STARED AT the main monitor, their noses almost touching the screen. The Winged Death was pulverizing any standing structure in the city—towers, parking garages, bridges, monuments—all fell to the space centaur.

"Hey, little buddy, looks like they're finally sending in the troops," Duke said to his ninja sidekick. "Let's see what the fabled military might of the ol' Earth is made of."

The bounty hunter turned around to see Lilly and Po'l both glued to ancillary monitors, watching the devastation, their mouths agape. The musk ox cringed as she watched the monster slam down its spiked tail on to a bridge, breaking it in two with as much ease as Ishiro'shea splitting a piece of plywood with his katana. She cleared her throat.

"Blop said he needed us—well, you, Duke—to save Earth. Are you sure about that? Don't get me wrong, I know you saved the universe and all, but this is a pretty big ask," she said.

Duke sighed.

"Yeah, I'm right there with you, Lil. I thought we'd be scufflin' with Mazilda and some Four I's flunkies. You woulda thought that Blop would have remembered to mention giant space behemoths," Duke responded. "I mean, don't get me wrong, I did save the—"

Ishiro'shea coughed at Duke.

"*We* did save the universe. And Admiral LePaco *did* have a weapon that would have flattened any living creature —even these three bastards—but at least he was, I don't know—"

"Smaller?" Po'l suggested.

"Yeah, I guess. We could take him out with a single shot. These cats won't be that easy."

"I'm hoping that won't even be necessary," said Lilly. "Maybe the Earth forces can do the heavy lifting."

"And we can get back to our mission," said the bounty hunter.

"What mission?" asked Po'l. "The walking mound of molding clay wanted us to save the Earth from Mazilda; the Yehaso did that for us. I say that we get out of here. The Blop was mistaken."

Ishiro'shea tapped Duke on the shoulder and directed his attention to the primary monitor. The Earth forces were arriving into the city.

They aren't messing around, thought Duke.

Though the Nova Texan was, by no means, an expert on Earth military vehicles—in fact, most non-Earthers weren't since the majority of Earth's military advancements were used on-planet against each other—but it was clear that what was rolling in was impressive.

The leaders appeared to have decided on a three-pronged approach, with assault teams arriving from the streets, from the river, and from the sky. There had to be thirty or forty assorted assault vehicles that were plowing through the smoldering debris of Chicago. And likely dozens more off-screen. Many were boxy and sturdy-looking, as if they were rolling gift boxes with wrapping paper made of five feet of reinforced steel. These cube tanks had massive cannons mounted to each side, protruding far beyond the front of the vehicle. But the really imposing element was the missile launching apparatus that sat on the top. It was a four-barrel missile deployment unit, nothing unusual or spectacular. In fact, it was a bit outdated in the scheme of ground-based battle vessels. Upon further examination, Duke noticed that the missiles were fake. Dummies. There for show.

"Holy hedgehogs, those are self-replicating pulse projectiles," Duke shouted. "That's some top-grade stuff."

"What's that?" asked the Neprian.

"Similar to the tech that powers Ol' Betsy—well, any gun suitable for *individual* use—these produce a never-ending supply of frickin' missiles. With maximum yield. Total relentless carnage. And they have twenty of them! I'm starting to feel better about our chances," said Duke, a smile creeping across his face.

Entering the screen, cutting through the bits of broken buildings and crushed bridges in the river, were a group of heavily armored ships. These weren't massive war ships; they would never have fit in the winding river that cut through the heart of Chicago, but they seemed to be able to pack a similar punch. Each ship was long and narrow with three mounted laser cannon stations on the top deck. At the rear of the ship, sitting on an elevated platform, was an armament that was unrecognizable to Duke. A mechanical cylinder extended from the platform and culminated in a transparent nozzle. It looked like a glass coffee mug. Numerous tubes and wires wound around the arm, covering the base, and ultimately, connecting into the nozzle.

I'm assuming that does something bad, concluded Duke.

The Winged Death hadn't seemed to notice the

approaching forces from the ground or river. But it did acknowledge the fighter ships that zipped by and peppered it with high intensity blasts. These attack cruisers were similar to the ones that had showed up in the final moments of the Great LePaco War. They could be pretty annoying to the most heavily armored ship and, apparently, to interstellar winged cyclops horses with eye lasers.

Four ships crisscrossed above the skyline, releasing quick, calculated pulses of pain upon the Winged Death. It covered its face with every passing strike. Another pass, more direct hits. No physical damage could be seen but it began to cocoon itself in its giant set of wings, using them as a shield. As the ships continued to engage with the monster, the ground units surrounded it. The ships remained at a distance, definitely close enough to strike, but not squarely in its imposing shadow.

It's being corralled, thought Duke.

Then the space creature extended its wings, knocking over two buildings in the process, and leapt into the air, narrowly avoiding the first round of pulse missiles from the cube tanks. It hovered in the air and let loose an eye beam that disintegrated one of the attack cruisers.

"It's pissed," muttered Duke. Now all four sets of eyes stared at the primary screen.

One of the spacecrafts whizzed towards the giant, lasers firing. But the monster swung its massive arm and connected with a clubbing right cross. The ship exploded like a firecracker.

The other two spacecrafts peeled away from the fight to seemingly regroup. The Winged Death hurled more eye lasers at the two, but none found their mark. After a brief hiatus, they circled back and headed in again. One of the ships pressed forward with a full artillery barrage aimed at the beast's face. The second ship swung around and attacked from the rear. The cube tanks and boats started to fire as well, pelting the Winged Death's flanks.

"Let's see how he likes this," cheered Duke. "The time for tickling this ghoul is over."

The Winged Death raised up so that all six limbs faced forward; in midair, it flapped its wings. This wasn't the smooth, effortless flaps that kept the beast afloat in the Chicago sky, this was a powerful, elongated whip. It was hard to tell from the monitors, but the gust had to be extremely powerful as the ship was blown off course from its valiant charge. Eye laser. The vessel was disintegrated.

The rear approaching ship advanced but was disemboweled unceremoniously by a well-placed tail strike; the three massive shards crashed into the underbelly of the vessel, splattering ship fragments across the city below.

"Holy hedgehogs, they need to send in more fighters. And now," said Duke. His colleagues' silence led him to believe that they agreed.

The Winged Death slowly descended back down to the war zone. As it returned to the Chicago street, its eye beams remained a relentless barrage on the ground and river forces. It landed with a boom. Its back leg shot backward, connecting with a rogue cube tank. The swift kick lifted the tank off the ground and flung it into the side of a mid-rise building in the northern part of the city. It flapped its wings with aggression again, causing an immense wind gust that toppled more buildings, some crashing into the legion of tanks. It reached down and grabbed a tank and hoisted it over his head. It slung the armored vehicle like a Mrelockian Mega-Troll throwing a particularly tiny pebble into the river. It smashed into one of the boats, erupting into a crimson fireball.

The Earth forces were turning into nothing more than a

nuisance. A bug bite on the backside of a three-headed ice wombat.

"Ish. There has to be a plan, right? Because, I hate to admit it, but I don't see this ending well," Duke proclaimed. "Man, I wish the Queen was here. I could use an inter-dimensional doomsday device right about now."

CHAPTER 15

YEHASO WITH THE SAVE

THE BOUNTY HUNTER HAD EXPECTED a more "secret" secret war room. It was just down the hall. With the door open. No guards. There was even a big sign that flashed "Secret War Room. Please Enter. But Only If You're Supposed to Be Here. We Practice the Honor Code."

Idiots, thought Duke LaGrange.

There were about twenty people in the room—General Munger, Colonel Tott, Ishiro's parents, assorted military personnel of various ranks, and in the back of the room, sitting in silence, were the Yehaso aliens.

Duke, Ishiro'shea, Lilly, and Po'l walked in.

There was a lot of shouting. A lot of red faces. A lot of panic. Most of it coming from Colonel Tott. The feisty officer turned and noticed the bounty hunter and his crew.

"Get out! How'd you find this place anyways? This is top secret!" he screamed.

"Really?" Duke countered.

The Father and Yumi shuffled over to the foursome and acted as a sort of barrier.

"Is he for real? Are you aware that there is a flashing

sign that says 'Secret War Room' outside? You can probably see it from orbit," said Duke.

"Calm down," the Father whispered. "Things aren't going as planned. This monster is a bit tougher than the General and the Colonel imagined. Any ideas?"

"Um," Duke stuttered, "I don't know...leave?"

"Not helpful, Duke," Yumi retorted. "How about you, son?"

The ninja shook his head.

"Anyone?" The Father asked.

Lilly and Po'l turned their gazes to the ground, shaking their heads.

"Look, we thought we were sent here to help stop Mazilda—not space monsters. Disgruntled middle management types with pulse pistols...the odd two-headed Jungafallowian foot soldier...those, we can take. They are right in our wheelhouse, ya' know. This thing right here with the wings and hooves and horn and eye lasers...we would be out of our depths," Duke explained.

"Have you asked the Yehaso?" asked Lilly calmly.

The group all paused. They looked at each other. It was the musk ox that broke the silence.

"That is why they're here, right? To help?"

The Father smiled and bowed at the Gartoshian. He pivoted and headed over to General Munger. It was too loud for anyone to make out what he said to the Earth officer but Munger seemed somewhat pleased. At least that's how Duke interpreted the General's stoic head nod.

"Thank you, Lilly," the Father said upon returning to the group. He quickly turned and headed towards the three beings sitting at the back of the room, watching the commotion expressionlessly. The Father ushered them to the head of the room.

"Everyone, silence!" shouted Munger. "Things got

carried away. Rushed decisions were made. I take full responsibility. I forgot that we have experts on this Winged Death. How do we defeat this?"

Venksplin rotated to the front position of the tightly packed trio.

"It is only a theory, General. We did not have time to test it out," the Yehaso spokesperson began.

"We'll take a theory at this point," replied Munger. "It's decimating our forces and hasn't even broken a sweat."

"Very well. We've theorized, based on some of the data we've collected and replaying the available footage from its attack on Yehaso, that the weak spot on the creature is the tip of the horn. We believe that there's a nerve center there that serves as the central hub for, not only its nervous system, but all of its cognitive processes. If it is attacked with significant force, it could force a retreat or render it immobile. Of course, this is only a theory."

Munger shifted her gaze to Colonel Tott.

"What are you waiting for, Colonel? Call it in. Air strike. Now! Tell whatever tanks and boats we've got out there to redirect all fire to that horn. Let's hope our Yehaso friends theorized right," said General Munger.

Most of the cube tanks were dismantled, nothing but smoldering hunks of twisted metal. The warships were either capsized, sunk, or retreating. The Winged Death had disposed of a sizable military force and flattened a city in the time it takes most life-forms to down a well-made martini. The Yehaso's theory about the beast was the only item on the docket before bigger and more ethically gray options had to be considered.

"Strike is ready, General," confirmed a soldier in the room.

"Ground support?" asked Munger.

"Yes, ma'am. We have a new wave of tanks surrounding

the city. We've upped the number. If this thing is even momentarily immobilized, it's going to eat a coordinated attack from fifty tanks and ten mounted electro-rays," the soldier added.

Po'l leaned in to Duke. "What's an electro-ray?"

"I didn't even know they still used those. Those have to be antiques," the bounty hunter began. "But think of it as a giant concentrated bolt of lightning that can be fired at something. It hurts, yes, but it's not as damaging as, say, a laser. A few planets in this sector used them, primarily on other big war machines. It would shut down most machines or, at the very least, make the controls go a bit haywire. Interesting choice to use them on an organic life-form."

"You don't think it's an android, like the Jungafallowian back on Psitakki, do you?" asked Lilly.

"Maybe," Duke replied, trying to block out the memories of the brutish Combatant 2 that terrorized opponents during the Tournament of the Shield of the Colossal Calamari. "I just hope the electric pulses don't make it stronger."

"We are confident that the concentrated electrical shocks will stun the beast; at least enough to keep it on the ground so we have a shot at mounting an attack on its horn," interjected General Munger, having obviously overheard the conversation.

"Makes sense," responded Po'l. Ishiro'shea bowed.

"We shall see, right?" Munger said as she walked away.

"ETA is one minute on the strike, General," said Colonel Tott. "Let's hope this works."

Duke looked at his ninja companion. "Hope is never a good strategy...militarily speaking."

Ishiro'shea nodded.

"But it is our most precious resource," countered Lilly.

Duke grinned.

"Yes, but when the Queen gave us that nugget of

wisdom, we were only facing off with an insane lunatic that had a universe swallowing inter-dimensional doomsday device and legions of pencil-pushing gunfighters. That was a piece of cake compared to this thing."

Before the Gartoshian could respond, the air strike commenced. It was quick, impressively so. Bobbing and weaving with an intricacy that Duke had never seen before with other militaries. Duke blinked and felt that he missed ten direct hits to the Winged Death's horn. The tanks and electro-rays began their onslaught as well, hoping to stabilize the beast and prevent it from fleeing into the sky. It appeared to be working. The beast was visibly shaken by the attack.

"Looks like your theory has legs," grumbled Colonel Tott to Venksplin and Lantejira. They did not respond. Their eyes remained glued to the screens. "Hey, where's the other one? I thought she'd like to see your plan in action."

Venksplin and Lantejira looked at each other. "Sattlamora? I am not sure where she is," began Venksplin. "Contrary to what you may think, we Yehaso are not bound at the hip."

"She's missing some good stuff," Tott replied.

The massive creature tried to cover itself with its wings in order to block the attack but timely blasts from the electro-rays kept pushing the wings open. The plan was working. Two attack ships dove in harmony from the sky and unleashed four mountain-blasting missiles to the chest of the Cosmos. Upon impact, the beast wobbled, then fell into a cluster of half-destroyed buildings. It was down. For the first time, it was down.

"Pounce on it! Now! Kill that bastard!" screamed General Munger. Her fists were clenched so tight that Duke expected her bones to burst through her skin at any minute.

The assault was relentless. The Winged Death squirmed and kicked but couldn't get back to its feet.

Then, without warning or a command from the General, some of the ground-based firing halted.

"What's going on?" asked Munger. "Why are they stopping?"

Then more tanks stopped firing.

"What's happening?" screamed Colonel Tott.

The screen panned down. Emerging from the river was a long serpentine neck. At the end was a reptilian face with an elongated snout, devious eyes, and teeth the size of tarzantia trees. More of its body exited the water and two front flippers—the size of the First Cosmos' wings—plopped down on the shoreline. It let out a wail that shook the ground. The tanks and electro-ray cannons that were in front of it were in flames. The sea monster straightened its neck, propelling its head towards an attack ship diving towards the fallen Cosmos. The Aqua Demon clamped down its powerful jaws on the ship. Immediately, the cruiser was engulfed in a blue flame, crashed into a building, and exploded on impact.

"Damnit. I forgot about the other two Cosmoses," said Duke.

CHAPTER 16

FROM CHICAGO TO LONDON

WITHIN MOMENTS AFTER ITS ARRIVAL, the Aqua Demon had altered the course of the skirmish in Chicago. The Winged Death was now back hovering over the city, blasting down any remaining structures with devastating eye bolts. The Aqua Demon had come fully onto the streets and, though obviously more comfortable in the water, it was no less destructive. Its massive wing-like foreflippers smothered entire neighborhoods with each piece of forward locomotion. It let loose a high-pitched, ear-piercing screech that morphed into a trumpeting call without transition.

"It's signaling something," Duke said to Ishiro'shea.

"You are correct, Duke LaGrange," cut in Venksplin. "Either to bring the last Cosmoses to Earth or for the two to move on to another destination."

"So what do we do?" asked the bounty hunter.

Before the Yehaso could respond, nearly everyone watching the demise of Chicago on the monitors gasped. Duke left the Yehaso and waded through the military officials to get a peek at whatever was causing such a reaction.

Chicago—what was left of it, anyways—was now ablaze.

Not a few fires here and there—no, it was full on, totally covered in flames.

"What happened?" Duke inquired.

"Not good, Duke," responded Po'l solemnly. "Not good at all."

"Did that big lizard hit a gas line or—"

On the screen, the Aqua Demon raised its torso up, balancing its behemoth body on its hind flippers. Its neck straightened momentarily and then its body came crashing down to the ground as it let loose a ball of fire that engulfed a third of the city.

"A monster that flies through space, lives under water, and breathes fire? Huh. Well, damn."

"And there are two other equally powerful creatures," added Sattlamora, having returned to the room.

Holy hedgehogs, don't creep up on me like that, thought Duke.

"Yeah, thanks for the reminder," replied the Nova Texan.

"General, updates," shouted Colonel Tott.

"Go on," Munger ordered.

"You aren't going to like them," Tott added, with noticeable reluctance in his voice.

"Colonel...the updates," Munger ordered again.

"It appears that the two beasts are leaving Chicago..."

"That's good," said Munger.

"...And heading east. At a rapid pace. The Winged Death is in the air, heading towards the coast. Possibly New York or Philadelphia or Newark. The Aqua Demon is entering Lake Michigan and its trajectory puts him at the Saint Lawrence Seaway in...wow, it's really fast...in a few moments. Minutes. That can't be right. No, it is. Minutes, General."

"Not so good," said Munger, remedying her initial reaction. "Let's reroute forces to the coast. They must want to get to the Atlantic. But why?"

"New Tokyo," replied the Father. "They're coming here."

The room fell silent.

Colonel Tott cleared his throat. "One more thing, General."

Munger said nothing; she merely dropped her head as if she was bracing for even more terrible news. She got it.

"The third monster. It's not on our screen anymore," said the Colonel.

Great, Blop placed me front and center for the demise of Earth. When I see that little wad of bubblegum again, I'm going to tell him to keep his damn omniscient thoughts to himself, thought Duke.

"We scanned Earth. If it's on the surface or in the air or in the water, it's not showing up," continued Tott. "Maybe it retreated."

"Retreated? Or realized it wasn't needed to lay waste to this rock?" whispered Duke. Ishiro'shea nodded in agreement.

"That could be the first piece of good news that we've had in a long time," Munger replied. "Yehaso, come here please."

The three aliens shuffled over methodically to the General.

"Do you have any tricks on how to hurt this sea lizard? The horn thing was working on the Winged Death before we were ambushed."

Sattlamora stepped forward.

"We do not. Our theories and hypotheses do not extend beyond the Winged Death."

Munger inhaled, her hands on her hips.

She looks lost, thought Duke.

"General," Tott began.

"Yes! What now, Colonel!" shouted the General.

"We found the third monster."

Though not as imposing or as important, politically speaking as its regional cousin New Tokyo, London was just as popular amongst those brave enough to visit Earth. Partly because it was rich in ancient Earth history but mostly because it was one of the few large cities on the planet that was somewhat safe. Despite being from Nova Texas, Duke was familiar with London; there was even a small town on Nova Texas called Londonia in honor of its settlers' original home. When the monitor switched over to a live feed of the city, his memories were quickly jarred by familiar images. The city looked as it did many cycles ago in his primary school classroom. Some of these structures had withstood millennia like the skyscrapers in Chicago—a bloody, chaos-riddled millennia, at that.

"Hey, hey, look at that, Ish, it's the clocktower thingy," shouted Duke, almost jovially. "I've always wanted to see that. Big Ben, right? And the Shard. And that, oh man, what's that funky cone building called?"

The ninja did not respond. No one did.

Well, I think it's pretty cool, Duke mused to himself.

"There, ma'am!" shouted one of the military technicians sitting at a control panel below the screens. "Look near the Gherkin, just south. I'll zoom in."

"The Gherkin! That's what it's called," Duke whispered to himself, smiling.

General Munger stood next to the officer as he enhanced the view on the screen. The image materialized clearly on the screen. It was a hole. A really big hole. The neighborhood that was once there was no more; just a collection of simmering bits of debris that dotted the outer rim of the trench.

"What type of explosion caused that?" the General asked. The room did not provide any answers.

"Something airborne. Something powerful. Do we have another one that can shoot some sort of laser from a body orifice? Keep those eyes on the skies," commanded Colonel Tott.

"Colonel, I don't think this is coming from the sky," responded the technician timidly.

At that moment, the area around the Gherkin began to visibly rumble on the screen. The bullet-shaped structure shook violently, fires and explosions springing up around its base. Dust and smoke consumed it immediately. The entire screen was rendered opaque.

"Zoom out," ordered General Munger. "What's happening?"

As the feed pulled back and provided a wider shot of the location, the thick cloud consuming the Gherkin towered over the city. It was an impressive site; a tightly wound tornado of dust and debris that stood taller than any other point in the ancient city.

"What's causing this?" the General continued. "It's imploding."

Before any additional commentary as to the cause of the demolition was muttered, a large horn emerged from the dust cloud. It was the size of an attack cruiser and curved upward like a scimitar. After the horn exited, then came the rest of the creature. Its body was built like an obsidian tank; sleek armor covered every aspect of its insectoid exoskeleton. The massive horn that extended from the tip of its head was mirrored by an even larger pronotal horn that curved downward. The beast came into clear view as the buildings around it, including the famed Gherkin, crashed to the ground, utterly ravaged. The Third Cosmos. The Underlord.

"It looks like a beetle," said Colonel Tott.

The Underlord let loose an earsplitting hiss into the foggy London air.

"It's answering them," said Lilly. "It's answering the other two. They're coordinating."

General Munger and Colonel Tott provided no counter.

"We have one thing going for us on this one, at least," began Colonel Tott. "This one can burrow but at least it doesn't spew fire or shoot lasers. It might make it easier to take down."

The behemoth beetle scurried across the city, knocking down or outright crushing anything in its path. It came to a sudden halt near Elizabeth Tower, the home of Big Ben. It let out another screech and an electric green slime exploded from its mouth. The blast covered the clock tower in the ooze. The emblem of the ancient city that had survived too many brutal and deadly wars to count slowly lost its structural integrity and caved in on itself. The concrete and metal infrastructure bubbled, the corrosive acid melting it away into nonexistence.

"You're right, Colonel. It doesn't shoot lasers," concluded Duke.

CHAPTER 17

AND IF THAT WASN'T
ENOUGH...

ONDON WAS DESTROYED. UTTERLY DESTROYED. What wasn't toppled over was melted down to unrecognizable yard art. Even through the images on the screen, Duke could feel the eeriness that overran the once great city. And the bug was scurrying out of town in a northwestern direction. Everyone in the room knew the Cosmos' destination. New Tokyo.

If the approach of an acid-vomiting space insect wasn't daunting enough, they had just been informed that the other two Cosmoses had been spotted in Dingle Bay on the southwestern edge of Ireland.

The room was silent. Duke knew that there were a lot of intelligent minds in that war room and some of their gears had to be turning; but whatever their brains were churning out didn't make it to their lips. The Father gripped his wife tightly and stared with vacant eyes at the screen showing the two monsters crush the quaint archaic town of Dingle. Every step seemed to flatten a different relic of the fishing village—a brightly colored pub here, a religious statue from Earth's bloody past there.

What a waste, thought Duke, as he remembered Cyborg Joe's, then his own quaint Queen Joe's back on Neprius.

Ishiro'shea sat on the floor next to his parents, legs crossed, eyes closed. He was deep in meditation. Po'l was glued to the screen, following the destructive path of the Third Cosmos, the Underlord, as it approached Luton. Before it reached the outskirts of the English city, it burrowed back under the ground and visual was lost on the behemoth beetle.

Lilly was pacing. This was new for the musk ox. She was usually the most calm of anyone in tense situations. She had seen a lot from her time on Gartosh—or rather the moon colonies of Gartosh—and played a pivotal role in the Great LePaco War, alongside her Gartoshian brethren. However, it was clear that she didn't have a plan to save a planet from a trio of planet-crushing space creatures. General Munger's eyes were darting frantically, from a view screen to one of her soldiers to the ceiling in no particular pattern or cadence. Her brain was either working double-time or she was going crazy. Duke hoped for the former. Her trusted wingman, Colonel Tott, was barking orders at anyone that walked in his line of sight. Most of it was unintelligible military babble; some of it was just plain mean.

But there they all were. In a small room, helplessly watching the entire countries of England and Ireland being ransacked. And there was nothing that they could do. Their attempts to corral or eliminate the beasts had proven fruitless, save for a small glimmer of hope on the Winged Death from when the Yehaso provided guidance on the beast's lone weakness. But even that failed as it prompted the emergence of the Aqua Demon. Nothing changed in the room for what seemed like hours. The Father and Yumi remained stoically embraced. Ishiro'shea meditated. Po'l stared. Lilly paced. Colonel Tott yelled. General Munger's eyes danced.

Duke thought they were stuck in a pan-dimensional time loop until the repetition was broken up by a young soldier who burst through the door. Her eyes were wide, her face was pale. But she wasn't fair-skinned. She was scared.

"General! General Munger!" she screamed.

The General snapped out of her daze and focused her attention on the stocky, redheaded Private. The soldier straightened up her torso, chest out, and saluted her superior.

"At ease, soldier," responded Munger. And the young Private's body relaxed. But the frightened look on her face remained. "What is it?"

"General, we've spotted something else."

"Who has?" the General retorted.

"We have," the Private reluctantly responded.

"We *who*? Everyone tracking the beasts is in this room, Private."

"Oh, this isn't a beast. Some of our troops stationed in Phuket, they reported that some spacecraft broke atmosphere and are heading...well..."

"Go on, Private," urged Munger.

"Here, ma'am."

Colonel Tott approached the conversation from the rear. His face was scowlier than ever.

"It probably was some of our ships, heading this way for help," he said dismissively.

"Colonel, they did not resemble any of our—" the Private began before being interrupted by the Colonel.

"So I'm to believe some split-second observation made by a part-time soldier, probably sloshed out of his mind on mai tais and daiquiris, floating on a sailboat in the Andaman Sea? I'm no fool, I know that base is more of a resort than it is a military outpost."

"We should have landed in Phuket," Duke whispered to

Ishiro'shea, still sitting cross-legged on the ground—but now with one eye open.

"Actually, Colonel, let's assume the Private's intel is correct," Munger replied. Tott did not like being undermined, even by his commanding officer. The young Private's cheeks quivered, preventing her from giving into that full-blown smile that pulsed under the surface. "Any other information on the ships?"

"Yes, General. They matched those of the recent force that attempted to invade. Mazilda Cloax's armada."

Duke's chest tightened and his stomach turned like a spinning top on a merry-go-round stuck in a cyclone.

"How many?"

"Not many, ma'am. A dozen or so, maybe twenty. But one did appear to be the vanguard ship from earlier," the Private continued.

Mazilda.

"Okay, Private. Have them route all intel up to the war room here. We need to know everything. And know it yesterday. Understand?"

The Private saluted and stormed out of the room as fast as she had burst in. She was a pretty girl. She reminded Duke a bit of Ja'a. Though Ja'a would never have been scared. Not in the face of a magic orb. Not in the face of astro-monsters. Not in the face of anything. Duke's mind could only think of his powerful and beautiful partner back on Neprius, rebuilding and leading an entire planet. Then he felt guilty for thinking that the Private was attractive.

What has happened to me?

"Let the few who survived our attack come. Let Mazilda Cloax come. They'll find that Earth has three surprises that they didn't account for. Either they get killed and all we have to do is find a way to destroy the monsters.

Or Mazilda kills the monsters and we can swoop in and defeat her again," said General Munger.

"Excellent plan, ma'am," echoed Colonel Tott.

"Yep, just that easy," Duke mumbled at Ishiro'shea, shaking his head. Lilly and Po'l both slid back so that they were both in between Duke and Ishiro.

"Yeah," began Lilly in a whisper, "we should probably have a plan B."

"And a plan C," added Po'l.

Duke knew he had the best crew in the whole of the universe.

CHAPTER 18

HOPE

"THEY JUST TOOK OUT ANOTHER squad of tanks," Colonel Tott said calmly to General Munger. "And some of our top fighters. In fact, anything that we send in from the air, Mazilda's fleet picks off. And if we send them after her people—"

"One of those damn monsters gets them," the General said, finishing Tott's thoughts. The Colonel nodded. "It's as if they are working together. But that's not, uh, it's not possible. It can't be."

"It appears that it is," Tott answered, his eyes fixated on the floor. After a lengthy pause, the Colonel asked, "Orders, General?"

After an equally lengthy pause, the General responded. "I...I don't know. Our forces are depleted. Whatever we send in won't last two minutes. I'm tired of ordering my people's deaths. We have our defense force here, it's our best hope. It's our *last* hope."

"I'd prefer to have three times more guns for those bastards," Tott countered.

Duke's mind kept wandering back to something the Queen said to him as they rushed headlong into a universe-altering conflict with Admiral LePaco. *Our most precious resource is hope.*

"Colonel, hope will do," the bounty hunter said with a smile. Both military officials looked at him quizzically. "I get it. On paper, this doesn't look so good. Somehow Mazilda and her minions found a way to control these three creatures. We don't know how. The Yehaso don't know how. But it happened, and we have to deal with it."

"Fine, fine, LaGrange. Your words are all fine and dandy, but they don't stop monsters the size of skyscrapers from destroying New Tokyo," the Colonel shot back.

"No, you're right, Colonel," replied Duke. "Words don't. But what words inspire can stop these monsters. Or anything. The city is evacuated, correct?"

General Munger nodded.

"Great. Let's use every trick in the book to slow these behemoths down. Electrified nets. Hidden ditches. The surprise nuclear bomb in the penthouse apartment. Whatever you can dream up, do it."

"We appreciate your help, bounty hunter," the Colonel began, his face twisted in annoyance, "but—"

"Let's hear him out," interjected the General.

"General?" Tott retorted. But Munger simply raised her hand in front of the Colonel and he ceased his opposition.

"We know that the Winged Death's horn is a weakness. Aim for it. Unless a fourth monster springs up, we won't be caught off guard. Do whatever you can to slow down the other two."

"That will work?" asked a lower-ranking soldier, standing behind Munger. The General was clearly not pleased with out-of-protocol questioning.

"No, not at all," Duke said with a grin. "If you happen to kill one, bonus points. But we want Mazilda and crew to think that we've doubled down on stopping the monsters."

"That will open us up for attack by Mazilda," replied another lower-ranking staff member. Murmurs and side conversations picked up in the war room. Munger's face grew red.

"Yes, but that's okay," answered Duke.

"Maybe for you," said one of the voices in the back.

"No, no, no. Calm down. See, it's a good thing if these monsters are truly being controlled by Mazilda or someone in her force. That means—first—that they *can* be controlled. And—more practically—it means that we can sever that control. So we let them think that they have a free pass at us, and we come in and cut off the head."

"We?" asked General Munger. "I thought the entire force would be concentrating on these Cosmoses?"

"We as in Duke LaGrange and my crew. And the *Deus Ex Machina*," Duke said triumphantly.

"You aren't soldiers in our military. You aren't even Earthborn," began Munger.

Ishiro'shea cleared his throat. It was lost on Munger.

"You do realize that we saved the universe, right?" Duke asked.

"Allegedly," the Colonel muttered.

The bounty hunter shook his head. "Well, we did. I feel that you can trust us to not screw up your 'mission.' And, even if we did, what real harm is it going to cause to anyone outside of us?"

The General and the Colonel turned their backs to Duke and his crew. They whispered in each other's ears for a few seconds and pivoted back towards Duke.

"Fine, we'll follow your plan," began the General. "We will concentrate our forces on the Cosmoses, and you will try and take out as many of Mazilda's ships as possible. Of course, we're hoping that the control mechanism is *on* one of those ships."

"Hope is our most precious resource," Duke said with a tip of his hat.

"One more thing, LaGrange," continued the General. "We want you to take the Yehaso."

"Really? Why?" replied Duke.

"They know the most about these creatures. Maybe they can provide some real-time direction as you're trying to swat spacecraft from the sky. We know they have great military minds; and you will need that for this 'mission,'" answered the General.

Duke turned to Ishiro and muttered out of the side of his mouth, "I should be offended, right?"

Ishiro'shea replied with a big thumbs-up.

"Colonel, get all of our defenses ready. Bring every living, breathing soldier on this part of the planet to New Tokyo. We are making our last stand," commanded Munger.

The war room was alive. Everyone doing some sort of job that, in theory, would aid in the defense of the city. Of their planet. Calls were being made. Coordinates being relayed. Plans being dealt. It was a frantic focus. It was what preparing for battle always felt like.

The General approached the four visitors. She leaned in.

"Are you sure? This is suicide. One ship against what? A dozen? Two dozen?"

"We don't have to take them all out, ma'am. Just the one that's controlling these beasts," Duke replied.

"If any of them are," she countered.

"Yes, we are hoping that's the case because our most precious—" began Duke.

"Yeah, yeah, yeah, hope. Precious resource. Got it," General Munger said. "I'm not a huge fan of letting outsiders lead high level missions where the fate of our planet is in the balance—"

"Does that happen a lot?" the bounty hunter asked with a grin.

Munger's eyes remained steely. "It's the second time in the—"

"Ah yes, the Yehaso. Sorry, forgot about that," said Duke. "And speaking of the Yehaso."

"Yes?"

"Where are they?"

They all looked around. No Yehaso.

CHAPTER 19

MISSING ALIENS

DUKE, ISHIRO'SHEA, LILLY, AND PO'L— accompanied by the Father and his wife, Yumi— sprinted down the nondescript hallway, weapons drawn. The General had sent out four different search parties to track down the missing trio of alien visitors. They weren't being picked up on any camera feeds and their bio signs weren't properly input into the system; they were essentially ghosts. However, when Duke asked if they had a camera monitoring their room—and received a "no" from Munger—he volunteered to take his team to inspect. *Probably just needed a nap*, thought Duke. But since the Yehaso weren't answering any of the attempts to reach them, the search party had to take every precaution necessary.

"It's just down this corridor," said Yumi. "On the right, the last door."

Ishiro's parents let the armed foursome take the lead. Duke slowly crept up to the open door and peeked around the doorframe. He signaled to his crew that what he saw—or didn't see—was inconclusive. He needed a better look. He motioned for Lilly to cover him.

The anthropomorphic musk ox shot back a quizzical look, followed by a hulking shoulder shrug.

"What?" whispered Duke.

"Cover you with what?" Fired back Lilly, in an equally silent tone. "My fists?"

Duke tossed her his laser revolver. He wasn't even sure if her hands were small enough to work it. *I'm sure she'll figure it out.*

The bounty hunter drew Ol' Betsy. He crouched down and then sprung into the entryway of the Yehaso's quarters. Lilly rotated in behind him. Ishiro'shea and Po'l followed, their blades in attack position.

"Empty," muttered Duke.

"And clean. Untouched," added Po'l.

"There has to be something," the bounty hunter began. "A note. A clue of some sort. Something."

"Or they just didn't come back to the room," said Lilly. "Maybe they went outside for a walk?"

"What? A leisurely stroll around New Tokyo? That'd be a first," snapped Duke.

"You saw it yourself, Duke, it looks much different now. It was green and quite striking," Lilly reminded the bounty hunter.

"We've made great improvements, Duke," chimed in Yumi, having now made her way into the room.

"Fine, fine, fine. I'm sure one of Munger's scouting parties went outside to see if they were out there, taking a smoke break and playing leapfrog or whatever," replied Duke.

The conversation was halted by the sound of gunfire. But not Earth guns. Duke knew those pulse sounds. *Four I's.* The barrage was followed by an even more unpleasant sound—the Father hitting the ground with a thud and a pain-riddled groan. Yumi shrieked. Ishiro'shea rushed to his father's aid, but the tough Irishman had already managed to crawl to safety. Duke leapt over the bleeding statesman and into the doorway. He saw four Four I's infantrymen at the other end of the hallway, trying to secure it. *But secure it for whom?*

"The General is going to kill me for this," Duke said as he pulled the trigger on Ol' Betsy. The Widowmaker let out a monstrous bellow that shook the walls in the corridor and culminated in a massive explosion at the other end. He didn't know if he hit anyone, but he definitely made whomever those troops were clearing a way for stop and think about continuing on. *If anything, the explosion should set off something in the war room and alert Munger to send help this way.*

"How is he?" Duke shouted back to the crew tending the Father.

"I'm fine," growled the Father. "They just nicked my shoulder. I've had a lot worse."

Duke peered back and saw that there was a steadily growing pool of blood on the floor, but the Father didn't look *too* bad. *He's a tough dude, no doubt.*

"Who were they?" asked Yumi.

"Four I's," answered Duke in a flat tone. "But I don't—"

Duke was interrupted by another round from the infantrymen, all aimed at him. Duke readied Betsy for another explosive greeting.

He peeked his head out again. Amongst the blazing fires and crumbled walls were a handful of Four I's soldiers. They waved on something. Or someone. *They're providing cover*, thought Duke. The bounty hunter decided not to return the volley. His curiosity was piqued. Were the Yehaso behind this? Then he saw them. The three aliens had their hands tied; and they were, in turn, tied together. Three Four I's soldiers led them by their biceps behind the wall of infantrymen rattling off pulses towards Duke and his crew. Behind the imprisoned aliens was someone that Duke did not recognize. And he looked like a badass. A badass cyborg.

"Hey, I found the Yehaso," Duke said back to the team without turning around. "But they appear to have been captured."

"Yeah, but it's just some Four I's. We've taken more of them out than this," replied Lilly, holding Duke's pulse pistol in the air.

"Not just Four I's. They have some cyborg leading 'em. Never seen him. Doesn't look cuddly, if you ask me." He peeked out again. "Yeah, not cuddly at all."

A loud explosion an arm's length from the door opening sent Duke backwards; he landed on his posterior in front of the Gartoshian musk ox. Lilly hoisted him up with ease.

"Let's trade," he said, handing Lilly his prized Betsy. "I don't want to kill the Yehaso too."

Duke twirled the laser revolver on his finger as he darted back to what remained of the doorframe.

"Cover me again," he yelled as he leapt from the doorframe and into a forward roll. Pulses splashed on either side of him, shooting up floor fragments. He returned fire, six pulses that took out the four infantrymen in the front and two of the three holding the Yehaso. No misses. The Yehaso remained frozen.

"Run, you morons!" Duke shouted at the alien trio. But they didn't budge.

The third Four I's soldier that was in charge of the prisoners aimed his rifle at the bounty hunter. Duke's eyes shot to the cyborg. His organic eye narrowed and his lips turned up one side. *Where's that cover*, Duke thought?

The gun exploded in the infantryman's hand. A throwing star landed between his eyes. He collapsed.

"Thanks, Ish," Duke said aloud to himself without looking back. "Not exactly the best cover in the universe but it worked. Let's just be happy that I didn't leave any more soldiers standing."

Ishiro'shea crept out from the room, his katana raised. Lilly followed with Betsy. Then Po'l, sword drawn. The quartet stared down the cyborg invader. There was a long silence.

"Seriously? Run, please. Now," Duke said, his frustration not well hidden. He jabbed his head to the side, just in case the Yehaso were having trouble understanding the language and needed more direct nonverbal clues.

Venksplin, Sattlamora, and Lantejira all moved to the side—still without as much a sense of urgency as the bounty hunter would have liked.

The cyborg did not try to flee. In fact, he walked towards them. No visible weapon. He raised his hands to hammer home this point. No one lowered their weapons. He stopped his approach about twenty paces from the group.

"Since when did the Four I's start employing cyborgs?" asked Duke.

"About the time that they realized the universe had a really bad bounty hunter infestation," snarled the cyborg.

"Did you happen to ask them about their record versus bounty hunters? You'll find that it's less than stellar," retorted Duke.

"They weren't paying me to get rid of them, then," replied the cyborg.

"Yes, all they had was a force three hundred times larger and an inter-dimensional doomsday device," scoffed the bounty hunter.

"Right, like I said, they didn't have me," the cyborg replied, his smile growing.

"Okay, enough friendly banter," interrupted Lilly. "Who are you? And what do you want with the Yehaso?"

"Is that what you call those grotesque pale skins?" the cyborg said, nodding towards the partially hidden alien trio. "Why would I tell you? Wouldn't that give you information that you could use against us?"

"Yes, but in my experience, you slimy, villainous bad guys do some really stupid things," Duke answered.

"Not this time. In fact, I think it's time for me to leave. Don't get me wrong, I give you all credit for stopping me. I'll admit when I fail. But the next time, you will die, Duke LaGrange."

How does he know who I am?

"Next time?" responded Po'l. "There won't be a next time."

The cyborg began to laugh. Duke re-aimed his pistol. Before he could pull the trigger, a violent explosion engulfed the ceiling. The force of the blast sent all four of them to the floor. The top of the hallway had been ripped off like a soggy bandage, exposing them to the cool Irish air.

Duke placed his forearm over his eyes to shield as much light as possible. He caught a glimpse of the cyborg ascending. Through the confusion, he heard the half man, half android scream, "I'll tell Mazilda that you said hello. I know she wanted to kill you herself, but it seems she will have to just enjoy watching the star beasts do it."

Well, that's how he knows me.

The Yehaso approached the shaken rescuers.

It was Sattlamora that extended a hand to Duke.

"Thank you for saving us," she said in a soft voice.

The bounty hunter did not respond immediately. His mind remained firmly fixated on Mazilda Cloax.

CHAPTER 20

PERSONAL GROWTH

"THAT'S AN INTERESTING TALE, LAGRANGE," said General Munger. "If my ceiling wasn't ripped off like the top of a tin can, I don't know if I'd believe you. But we are in the middle of dealing with surviving remnants of the Four I's and three rampaging cosmic monsters...so a death-defying flying cyborg isn't totally asinine."

"I don't think he actually flew," Duke gasped. "I'm sure he was on a rope or something."

The General did not pay attention to the bounty hunter's clarification.

"Are y'all okay?" the General asked the Yehaso.

They all nodded in unison.

"Any idea on why they would seek you three out, specifically?" she inquired further.

"Maybe they knew that they were the brains behind the first attack that drove them away?" commented Duke. "Maybe they think we aren't much without them, pulling the strings."

Colonel Tott growled at the bounty hunter but the General seemed to ponder it.

"Possibly," she said. Tott's face reddened.

"I don't think that is the reason," Venksplin interjected. Sattlamora quickly grabbed him, in the first real showing of disagreement between the three inseparable aliens.

"It's not worth it, Venksplin," Lantejira added, in something resembling a yell. "It will only bring more trouble."

He turned back to them, his face somehow even more pale.

"No, they need to know," Venksplin said. "The enemy came here to get us because of this. You know it. I know it. We must tell them."

"You don't know that's why, Venksplin," pleaded Sattlamora. "It's only a guess."

"They must know," Venksplin demanded. The other two Yehaso stepped back.

"Hey guys," Duke interrupted. "You do know that we're just right over here, right? What in the name of Nova Texas is going on?"

"Yeah, I agree with LaGrange," added Colonel Tott. "And that probably won't happen again. Ever."

"We might have an idea as to why Mazilda Cloax and her forces attempted to capture us," began Venksplin.

"It's just an idea," Sattlamora added. "We don't know for sure."

Venksplin shot her a glance.

"It isn't confirmed but I'm—*we*—are confident that this is likely the reason. Since the first appearance of the Cosmoses back on our home world, we have experimented with a serum. A serum that would possibly kill the beasts."

"And you haven't found it necessary to tell us this," screamed Colonel Tott. "Are you kidding me?"

A rousing grumble grew amongst those in the room. It escalated quickly to a full-on angry commotion.

"Please let me finish," pleaded Venksplin. "There

doesn't exist a poison or serum that can simply kill the monsters. Or even slow them down."

"Now I'm confused," responded General Munger. "A serum that can kill them but not kill them? Please elaborate for the sake of the Earth."

"This serum can make the entity that consumes it..." Venksplin paused. "...It can make them grow."

Silence.

"Really big," added Sattlamora, extending her arms to support the claim.

"The subjects would grow to the same size as the Cosmoses," concluded Venksplin.

"And then what?" asked Colonel Tott.

"Then, they could engage the Cosmoses in battle," answered Venksplin.

The silence continued. Then a slight giggle emerged from the back. Then another. Laughter broke out.

"A magic growing potion?" asked Colonel Tott.

"In theory," said Venksplin. "It hasn't proven itself to be successful on most occasions. And when it is—and the subject survives—the gigantism is temporary. An Earth hour, tops."

"A magic growing potion that doesn't even work most of the time," the Colonel clarified. "And that's why they came to kidnap you?"

"We believe so," said Venksplin.

The laughter simmered but Duke could still feel the eye rolls and headshakes from the Earth soldiers despite not being able to see them. He did not share in their humorous moment. He glanced at Ishiro'shea. Then at Lilly. And at Po'l. They seemed to miss the joke as well. *At least we're all on the same page.*

Yumi stepped in front of the Colonel.

"My Yehaso friends, did the cyborg take this serum? Do they have it?" she asked.

The Yehaso trio exchanged glances, all shaking their heads at one another.

"It appears not," Venksplin answered.

Lantejira reached into his tunic and revealed a vial containing a dark liquid. Sattlamora did the same. Venksplin revealed two identical bottles.

Looks like whiskey, thought Duke.

"That's good," Yumi said, accompanied by a courteous bow.

"Oh is it?" mocked Colonel Tott. "We wouldn't want to miss out on our opportunity to make a building-sized Duke LaGrange!"

"We would have to refine the serum to make sure that it works, anyway," added Venksplin.

"He wasn't being serious," whispered Duke to the Yehaso.

"Oh. But I was," he countered.

We can work on sarcasm at a later date, concluded Duke.

"Can you imagine a bunch of giants trying to beat up those monsters? If that's our best shot, we are already doomed," said the Colonel.

"Sirs," interjected a voice. It was the scarlet-headed Private. "A squad of Mazilda's fighters is closing in on New Tokyo. The big bug is already at Bray. The dinosaur thing is in Dublin Bay. And the flying one is hovering over the town as we speak."

"Orders, General?" Tott asked Munger. The General said nothing.

It was the Nova Texan who broke the silence.

"We got it, General," he said.

"What are you talking—" she paused.

Ishiro'shea stood next to the bounty hunter, all four bottles of serum balanced in his arms.

"He is a ninja, remember?" Duke said to no one in particular.

Po'l grabbed one of the smaller bottles and chugged it. Lilly did the same. Ishiro'shea gulped down half of the larger bottle that Venksplin possessed. He passed it to Duke.

"Looks like we're going to save the day. Again. Cheers." The bounty hunter finished off the liquid.

That burns. Sure doesn't taste like whiskey.

The Yehaso said nothing. The Earth leaders said nothing.

"Lilly, go south. Po'l, head towards the bay. Ish, you and I will get to a clearing near the city so we can draw the Winged Death and the spacecraft out of the city center," Duke commanded. They all headed for the exit.

"How long until we get...ya' know...big?" Duke asked Venksplin, his face still holding the same expression from learning that their serum was stolen from their very clutches, under their very noses.

"Soon. A few Earth minutes. Maybe ten. Fifteen, tops," answered the smallest Yehaso.

"Thanks," answered Duke. "And Earth...you're welcome."

CHAPTER 21

LILLY & THE UNDERLORD

"**P**LEASE TELL ME THIS WILL work," the Father asked the Yehaso.

All three looked at each other, eyes wide and darting frantically.

"We don't know," said Venksplin. "It will either work..."

"Or it won't," finished Lantejira. "We have not had a great success rate but then again, we've only tested the serum on Yehaso—and an occasional subspecies from our system. Never an Earther. Or a Nova Texan. Or a Gartoshian. Or a..."

"Primitive humanoid," concluded Sattlamora.

"I see," the Father replied, turning to his wife. Yumi clung to his arm. She was always so strong, so resolved and steadfast, even during the harshest of conflicts and the toughest of decisions. But she was sobbing uncontrollably.

"We can't lose him again. We just got him back," she cried.

"Yumi, you know for a fact that if he didn't take that potion, *we* would have. He is *our* son," the Father explained.

"It should have been us! It should have been us!" she bellowed.

The war room was frenetic; many were scrambling about trying to understand what was happening outside, others were trying to get their personal affairs in order as the three beasts and a Four I's armada made their way to New Tokyo.

"I got something," screamed a soldier from the back. "I've spotted the Gartoshian. She's in...she's near Bray?"

The entire room shifted from frenetic to a confused chaos.

"It worked," the Father whispered through a smile. "The potion worked. Look at her."

"On Lilly. We don't know about the others," Yumi replied, seemingly unfazed by the now Cosmos-sized musk ox. She released the Father's arm. "Any word on the other three?"

"I don't have anything yet. If they're giants, they're awfully small giants," the unseen soldier responded.

Everyone huddled around the largest screen in the room, watching the unbelievable. The Father scanned the walls and noticed an unoccupied monitor in the back corner. They both approached the screen and, though there was no true relief from the noise of the room, they were able to block some of it out as they huddled in front of the monitor.

"Where's this feed coming from?" asked Yumi. "It doesn't seem like an official broadcast or newsfeed."

"Munger mentioned that they had a military installation in Bray; I think they were deployed here to help fortify New Tokyo. My guess is that it's a network of surveillance and security cameras that are all synched," replied the Father. "Why is this the only monitor tapped into it? That, I have no idea."

"I'm so worried," Yumi pleaded. "I just don't trust this

option, this potion. The Yehaso didn't and that makes me nervous."

"If anyone can survive it, it's a Gartoshian. They are the toughest species I've ever met," answered the Father.

"That's what I'm worried about," Yumi answered. Her eyes looked at the ground.

"Ishiro'shea will be fine, my love. He has too much of you in him to let some silly potion bring him down."

The Father embraced his wife, tears now streaming down her cheeks.

"I guess I have to have faith in our son."

"We had faith that, even without us, he would live a fulfilling life. And look what happened. He saved the universe," said the Father.

"Yes, but he also owns a bar," she countered, a smile prodding through the sadness. Her husband grabbed her tighter.

Their attention quickly turned back to the screen. The cliffs of Bray exploded. Large chunks of rock shot miles into the Irish Sea. Despite the noise in the room and the relatively low volume of the camera feed, the earsplitting hiss rattled the Father's eardrums. His wife covered her ears. As the cliffs crumbled into their watery home, two horns burst through into the sunlit coastal beauty of Bray. The Underlord shook its segmented head as it breached, debris flying across the landscape. It let out another hiss. The cosmic beetle exited the tunnel that it had created and headed toward the city center. It headed toward the recently jumbo-sized Gartoshian.

The musk ox, now as tall as any of the three Cosmoses, stood on the edge of Bray, the city at her back. The Underlord stared her down, across a sprawling tapestry of hills, dotted with clusters of Scots pines. Lilly firmed her stance and clenched her fists. Her nostrils pulsated as her eyes narrowed on her opponent. The Underlord twisted its head, flashing its immense horns. Its wings, covering its back in the form of an impenetrable shell, lifted and fluttered. The cosmic insect let out a third screech and vaulted itself into the air. Its wings extended, and it shot horn-first at the giant Gartoshian. Lilly pounded her fist into her open palm as she anticipated the monstrous missile. She readied for impact but the Underlord veered away from the projected point of impact, out of Lilly's reach, and released a mouthful of radiating green slime. It struck the musk ox in the shoulder. Her exposed fur sizzled and smoked upon contact and she fell to the ground.

The Underlord landed safely and crawled toward its opponent, who was wincing in pain. It released another volley of toxic spit. Lilly rolled away and the venom covered a patch of pines, reducing them to ash as quick as a sunset on Ecclox. Lilly made her way to her feet, still clutching her shoulder. But as soon as she was upright, she was struck by the bolting Underlord's pronotal horn square in the chest, sending her back down to the ground.

"This beast is killing her," screamed Yumi.

The Father said nothing. He tightened his embrace and continued to watch the two goliath combatants do battle.

The Underlord hissed again, this time sounding more like a series of truncated trumpets. It continued the calls until Lilly staggered up again. The trumpeting halted and the beetle turned himself into a projectile once again. Lilly struggled to get her two feet under her, balancing with her left hand on the ground.

"She doesn't even see it," shouted Yumi. She turned her head.

The Underlord approached the shaken Gartoshian, readying for the kill shot. But Lilly rolled to the side, avoiding the strike path, then leapt in the air and grabbed the beetle's two horns. The weight of the Gartoshian brought the bug crashing down to the Bray countryside.

She was playing possum, thought the Father.

The Underlord was trying to flip over from its back as Lilly approached. She took both hands and gripped the pronotal horn. As she squeezed, she grimaced as smoke still bellowed from the wound on her shoulder. She began to drag the Underlord until she had enough momentum to lift him from the ground. She began to move in a circular motion, swinging the space beast. Just as she built up speed, she released the monster and it spun through the air uncontrollably until it crashed into the slope of a hill. The entire mound of earth detonated on impact, the resulting debris covering the monster.

Lilly sprinted toward the downed creature. As she neared the submerged Cosmos, she leapt in the air with a clenched fist raised. Her powerful right hand crashed through the pile of rock.

"That had to kill it, right?" The Father muttered.

"It had to," answered his wife.

Lilly stood up and her face gave them the true answer. She began to dig through the deconstructed hill, tossing dirt and rocks frantically into the air.

It's burrowing, thought the Father.

"Turn around!" shouted Yumi at the monitor.

The Underlord came up from the ground behind the musk ox and struck Lilly in the back with the broadside of its horn. She was lifted into the air and landed on her injured shoulder. The bug shuffled toward the Gartoshian. Before reaching Lilly, it raised itself on its hind legs and let loose an even more sound-defying squeal. Lilly lifted herself up as the Underlord looked to the sky; she lunged toward the exposed underbelly of the monster. She threw a vicious right cross that connected flush with the underside of the beetle's thorax. Upon contact, toxic slime flew out of the Underlord's mouth as it hit the ground with great impact. Lilly instantly collapsed.

Neither Lilly nor the Cosmos moved for a minute.

Are they both dead? the Father asked himself.

The back legs of the Underlord began to twitch. Then it began to move, laboring with every step. It stumbled, like a geriatric roller skater on a patch of gravel, toward the Irish Sea. As it made its way to the cliff, its legs gave out and it tumbled over the edge and into the water.

The camera feed panned back to the injured Gartoshian. But she was gone.

"Where is she?" the Father shouted.

Yumi inched closer to the monitor. She tapped it.

"There," she said.

"There's nothing there, Yumi."

"Nothing giant-sized, no. But she's there. That speck is Lilly. She's back to normal size," Yumi explained. She scanned the walls until her eyes fixated on a digital readout of the time. "And the potion lasted about forty-two minutes."

The Father hugged his wife again, this time even tighter than the previous one. Without releasing her, he turned to the crowd gathered around the primary monitor.

"General," he began in a booming tone, "get your men to Bray and bring back that musk ox."

CHAPTER 22

PO'L & THE AQUA DEMON

T HE GENERAL BARKED ORDERS AT her subordinates; they scrambled to piece together a rescue party for the now normal-sized musk ox who was passed out in a field outside of Bray. The commotion caused the Father to forget about the other three who had taken the Yehaso potion, including his own son. But that quickly changed.

"Sirs," shouted a soldier, "we have another report. Looks like one of the others has grown."

"Patch it in," shouted Munger. "Main screen. Who is it, Private?"

"The primitive, ma'am," he responded.

Before the Father could breathe a sigh of relief, Po'l, now as tall as a building, was on the main monitor. All eyes locked in on the Neprian warrior.

"Shouldn't he be naked?" asked Yumi aloud. "His clothes grew too."

It was Venksplin that appeared, seemingly out of nowhere, and spoke.

"There is much that we do not know about this potion and its effects. We have theorized that it will enlarge anything touching the subject, but ample tests have not been administered."

"We should have told him to not drop his sword," replied the Father.

"He's near the bay," interrupted the Private.

"You don't think we can see that?" hissed Colonel Tott. "We are familiar with this area, after all."

"Sorry, sir," replied the Private in a dejected tone.

Po'l was indeed at the bay, and on the very edge of the water. He knelt down to examine it in more detail. His head veered back and forth, his eyes equally as jittery. He stepped in, each leg as big as a redwood tree, each step creating a tidal wave that spilled out onto the shore. He plunged his entire arm into the suddenly turbulent water. A moment later, he lifted it. But his grasp held nothing. He repeated the same gesture. Again empty. He waded out farther into the bay, continually stabbing at the water with his gargantuan arm.

Yumi grabbed her husband's arm tightly and looked up at him.

"I have a bad feeling about this," she said. "If that thing is—"

Suddenly, the Neprian giant was sucked under the water. A collective gasp filled the war room. Yumi squeezed so hard that the Father thought his arm might snap.

"Where is he?" screamed General Munger at no one in particular. Regardless, people scrambled to their control panels as if pushing a few buttons would make Po'l suddenly rise from his watery cage. "Any eyes on him?"

No one responded.

Finally, Colonel Tott replied nonchalantly, "I hope he can swim."

The Father's eyes caught Yumi's and he simply mouthed, "don't." He could sense the fire in his spouse.

Activity began to commence in the bay, near the shore-line. Waves reached the height of the nearby mid-rises that overlooked the scenic bay, and they toppled onto the shore, immediately placing the local roads underwater. The commotion intensified until the long reptilian neck of the Aqua Demon emerged, mouth raised to the sky, trumpeting a haunting bellow that produced intermittent puffs of fire. The Aqua Demon's neck and head swung violently like a marionette whose operator was having a seizure. It flailed about, numerous balls of fiery spit landing in the middle of what once was luxury bayside real estate.

"What's wrong with that thing?" asked Colonel Tott. "Did it eat the primitive?"

They received the answer immediately.

As the Aqua Demon's body emerged from the water, on its back and riding it like a wild Mrelockian sky beast was Po'l. The colossal Neprian was holding on as the monster jerked and contorted its body to try and rid itself of the primitive humanoid. When the beast reached the pinnacle of a buck, Po'l would pound his clenched fists against its sides with powerful body blows and regain his grip as the beast plunged downward. It was hard to tell the physical impact that the Neprian's punches had on the Aqua Demon, but the struggle did accomplish one thing—the monster was slowly being guided to the shore.

As they reached the shallow waters of the bay, Po'l was flung unceremoniously into a cluster of buildings. The monster exited the turbulent waters and darted towards its downed opponent, each foreflipper strike shaking the ground. Po'l struggled to his feet, using the decimated remains of an apartment complex to gain stability. As he got his body upright, the charging titan extended his neck and let loose a massive stream of fire. Po'l dropped to his stomach, flattening a park in the process, and the flames ripped over him, and covered a previously undamaged set of high rises. Within moments, they had toppled over.

The Aqua Demon rose up on his hind flippers, coiled his neck back, and readied for another salvo of fiery destruction. But Po'l was already up and propelled himself like a missile at the monster's underside. He tackled the beast, sending both back into the shallow waters. The Aqua Demon was clearly not used to being manhandled in this fashion. Its trumpets now sounded more like distress calls than the triumphant bawls of victory. The Neprian, still holding on to the Cosmos' torso, dead lifted the beast out of the water and slung him back on the shore. Po'l leapt into the air and came down with a hard strike to the gut of the monster. It was clearly in pain. Straddled over the beast, Po'l went for another strike but it never landed; the Aqua Demon's massive foreflipper swatted the Neprian giant, sending him to the ground.

The monster flipped over and rose again to discharge another fireball. The flames shot out of the sea dragon's open jaws as Po'l rushed towards it. The lower half of the beam connected with Po'l's right bicep as the majority of the blast continued until it enveloped a communication tower at the edge of the town. Po'l did not slow down his approach as the fire continued to scorch his arm. In one fluid motion, he crouched below the outstretched neck of the monster and jammed his flame-covered arm into the beast's exposed chest. But Po'l held on to its torso, lifting it in the process, and vaulting both himself and the Aqua Demon back into the bay. As they hit the water, Po'l's entire back was now engulfed in flames. Their impact sent massive waves skywards before crashing back down where the giant humanoid and sea monster had entered the bay.

Moments slowly passed in the war room.

"Anything, Private?" barked Tott.

"Nothing, sir. Wait. We are picking up something leaving the bay at a rapid speed," the soldier responded.

The Aqua Demon, concluded the Father.

"It's the Cosmos. No sign of the primitive," the soldier added.

"His name is Po'l," shouted Yumi.

Tott shot an icy glance back at Ishiro'shea's mother but she did not waver. Her daggers were just as sharp as the abrasive Colonel.

"Same team, dear," the Father whispered to his wife.

"I don't care for him," she replied back, out of earshot of the Colonel.

"Oh, wait, Colonel. I have something. On the shore. I believe that's the primitive. He appears to be alive," the Private exclaimed. "Should we send a rescue team?"

"Yes!" interjected Yumi.

The Colonel chose not to stare down the proud ancestor of Takeo Nobunaga.

"Call it in," Tott grumbled.

CHAPTER 23

ISHIRO'SHEA & THE WINGED DEATH

"WE HAVE THE LITTLE GREEN one on the scanner," proclaimed Tott with a smirk. "And the Winged Death. Outside of New Tokyo but too close to us for my liking."

"He's doing that on purpose, just to get under my skin. He knows his name," said Yumi to her husband.

"I know. Just ignore it. Let's just be happy that Ishiro'shea is alive. How long did Lilly stay grown again?" asked the Father.

"Forty-two minutes," replied Yumi.

"And Po'l?"

"Sixty-four in total. Based on our estimates when he actually reached that size," Yumi answered again. "I guess different species react differently to the elixir. If Ishiro'shea grew around the same time, he'd be close to eighty minutes now. But I think it might have been delayed, otherwise, the scanner would have picked him up, right?"

"That makes sense," said the Father. "We are dealing with an unknown science, so let's just pray that he can stay this size long enough to damage that flying brute. Assuming the monster engages."

The main screen in the war room was squarely focused on a swath of land just outside of New Tokyo. In the middle of a clearing was Ishiro'shea, meditating. He was only a few paces from the edge of an industrial area of New Tokyo littered with factories and refineries. Clearly, this area had not realized the beautification to the degree of the more populous city center. Across his giant-sized lap was a giant-sized katana.

Thank God he held on to his sword, thought the Father.

Colonel Tott positioned himself in front of the primary screen, his hands clasped behind his back. "Okay, we have eyes on three of them. What about LaGrange? Do we think the Yehaso killed him with their potion?"

Before any of the rank-and-file could respond to the gruff commander, everyone's attention was brought back to the primary feed. Raining down from above was a beam; as it moved through the industrial area, the factories were exploding one by one, causing bright clouds of fire to cover the Irish sky. The beam continued toward the meditating ninja, creating a chasm in the ground as it went. Before it made contact with Ishiro'shea, the ninja sprang out of the way and rolled out of its path. He drew his katana and ran away from the direction of the beam, towards the city center.

"Why is he heading this way?" shouted Tott. "Why would he direct fire at us?"

Ishiro'shea picked up speed as he approached the impressive skyline of New Tokyo. He leapt in the air, his right foot landing atop one of the shorter buildings, then without so much as displacing a roofing tile, vaulted to a slightly taller building. Within a flash, the gargantuan ninja was atop the tallest building in New Tokyo, readying for a strike.

The beam had briefly stopped but then it reappeared,

cutting through the upper third of the super skyscraper where Ishiro'shea was perched. As his stoop exploded, the ninja leapt high into the clouds and out of the range of the monitor.

A mere second later, the Winged Death was falling rapidly to the ground with Ishiro'shea on its back, twisting its neck to redirect its eye beam away from New Tokyo.

"Brace for impact!" screamed Tott.

Ishiro'shea and the Winged Death crashed to the ground, outside of the city.

The war room felt only a tiny tremble.

"He steered that thing outside the city on the descent," the Father told Yumi.

Ishiro'shea and the space centaur regained their composures simultaneously. The centaur reared back and let loose another eye beam. Ishiro'shea dodged it and came up with a swift katana swipe to the Cosmos' left wing. It sliced through with ease. The Winged Death's painful cry shattered the majority of the windows in the city center. As Ishiro'shea turned to attack again, he was met with the back hoof of the monster. The blow sent Ishiro'shea to the ground, clutching his chest. With his free arm, he grabbed his katana and slung it towards the beast. The Winged Death's eye beam connected with the sword, halting its advance and sending it blade-first into the Irish soil. The titan launched another beam barrage but Ishiro'shea narrowly avoided it. It was clear that the ninja was injured from the beast's violent kick, and he wouldn't be able to avoid the onslaught forever. The monster rushed towards the injured ninja, raised up, and tried to crush him with his front hooves. Ishiro'shea rolled under the centaur, got to his feet, and leapt on his back. He straddled the back and hooked in a choke hold. The four-fingered claws of the Cosmos tried to free itself from the choke, but Ishiro'shea had it cinched in. It writhed and rolled but the ninja did not loosen his grip. Finally, the monster took to the sky.

It was obvious that the damaged wing was affecting the beast's flying abilities. It would gain altitude and then plummet into a chaotic free fall before regaining inertial stability. This happened over and over. Finally, its wings went limp. The descent was rapid, and the ninja had no means of controlling the fall. The duo's path led into a dense configuration of burning factories, just outside the city center.

"Son!" screamed the Father.

They hit the buildings and a single explosion covered the industrial neighborhood with an umbrella of fire.

"No! Ishiro!" cried Yumi as she embraced her husband.

There was no movement. The entire war room was silent.

Then a flitter. Rising above the intense fire was the damaged wing of the Cosmos. It rolled to its feet and vaulted itself into the sky. It about-faced and hovered over the ninja.

"It's going to shoot him with the beam!" shouted an unseen soldier in the war room.

A shimmering object emerged from the blaze and struck the monster. It was a throwing star. One of Ishiro'shea's throwing stars. The projectile buried itself in the monster's horn, where the Yehaso had instructed them to focus their efforts. The Winged Death howled again and retreated into the clouds in an erratic pattern.

The still giant Ishiro'shea crawled away from the fiery wreckage of New Tokyo and into the clearing. He assumed his meditative position. Moments later, the battered ninja was his normal size.

CHAPTER 24

A DAY AT THE PARK

A DESERTED NEW TOKYO JUST didn't feel right. As Duke sauntered down countless empty alleyways in the city center, he couldn't help but think about his three comrades. Po'l headed towards Dublin Bay, Lilly to Bray, and Ishiro'shea to the other side of New Tokyo. Surely, if his ninja companion had grown to be the size of a monster, he would have seen or heard it by now. They had only been out of the war room for fifteen or twenty minutes, and nothing. He was the same size as he was when he took a shot of the Yehaso's supposed miracle concoction.

Aside from the lack of a manufactured mega-growth spurt, he hadn't heard a peep from the Winged Death—which was presumably hovering over the city—or the Four I's fleet that was apparently closing in.

Did Tott's minions misread the situation? thought Duke.

The bounty hunter continued his uneventful stroll to the east side of the city center. More alleys. More alleyways. More nothing. He pulled out his communicator and punched in a code.

"Father. Yumi. You copy?" Duke asked.

"Yes, Duke. We're here. You won't believe what we just saw," replied the Irishman.

"I'm all ears. It's a bit boring down here on patrol. And I'm still the size of, well, me," Duke replied.

"Lilly and Po'l just went toe to toe with two of the Cosmoses," Yumi shouted.

"And?"

"And we can call it a draw. They drove the beasts away but they both shrunk down relatively quickly," the Father replied.

"How quick is 'quickly,' in your books?" asked Duke.

"Lilly's wore off in about forty-two minutes, give or take. Po'l's lasted longer, we think, by about twenty minutes," replied Yumi. "It's hard to tell since we didn't see him actually grow. It could've been delayed."

"Like mine," mumbled Duke.

"And we haven't seen Ishiro'shea yet," interjected the Father. "But at least the Winged Death hasn't shown up either. We've scanned the entire west side but nothing yet."

"I'm guessing that Earth humans and descendants of Earth humans might have a delayed reaction to this stuff or, worst case, no reaction," the bounty hunter surmised. "Then again, I guess the worst case would be that it kills us so it's not all bad. Yet."

The transmission crackled.

"You there?" asked Duke. "Still hear me?"

"Duke, we're losing you. But Tott just found Ishiro'shea. We're going to go, good luck and be safe," stated the Father.

"Keep me updated. I should see or hear something down here," responded Duke. "I mean—"

A beam of light cut through the overcast skies, its target clearly the industrial sector of New Tokyo to the west.

Winged Death, thought Duke. *And giant Ish. Holy hedgehogs, I better get out of here.*

Duke could hear the explosions from the factories; each one resulted in tremors that shook the concrete under Duke's feet. It made it more difficult to run but the bounty hunter managed to sprint for a full ten minutes. He wasn't out of the city entirely, but the combusting factories were very much out of range.

However, despite distancing himself from the action, Duke knew that it would only take a few steps for a giant ninja or a few flaps of its wings for a titanic space centaur and they would be on top of him. Or, worse, he would be under a toppling building—and he still was standing in the shadows of some of the tallest buildings in Ireland.

After a short respite, Duke continued out of the city, eyes peeled for Mazilda's fleet. If he wasn't a giant, he could still take some potshots with Ol' Betsy at some of the cruisers, assuming they flew low enough. At this idea, he holstered his laser revolver and took up arms with his Widowmaker shotgun.

The bounty hunter entered one of the newly installed parks. It was a lovely place, with pristine greenery and a babbling brook flowing through a field of wildflowers. Playgrounds to the right, picnic tables to the left, and a stage for outdoor performances tucked under a grove of sycamore trees. *I hate outdoor theater*, thought Duke.

Because of his disdain for outdoor theater, the bounty hunter had mixed feelings about what unfolded immediately after he entered the park. He felt the *whoosh* of a battle cruiser overhead before he heard the whine of the darting spacecraft. It turned around and opened up a series of laser pulses aimed at the bounty hunter. The first round shattered the stage and reduced the grove of sycamore trees to a scorched pile of dust. Three more battle cruisers appeared over the park. Then a few attack class scout ships behind them. Duke turned around and noticed five more ships, all different makes and models. One was definitely a Jungafallowian Fighter ship. The others could have been from any number of mercenaries that didn't care for bounty hunters or Duke LaGrange or anything, when paid properly.

Appearing above the last row of scout ships was a beautiful spacecraft, lush and extravagant and deadly. It had an impressive set of visible armaments and, Duke assumed, even more death-dealing tools concealed from view.

That's Mazilda, Duke thought to himself. *That's the ship that's coordinating all of this.*

One of the battle cruisers fired another pulse at the park, destroying a peaceful pagoda that stood at the banks of the brook. The wood shot in every direction from the explosion, one piece landing mere inches from the bounty hunter. Duke ducked for cover, dropping Ol' Betsy into the soft grass.

The battle cruisers and scout ships peeled away, providing a direct path for the impressive lead ship to make its way towards the bounty hunter. Duke searched around for Ol' Betsy but then stopped and clutched his stomach.

Not the time to get sick, Duke, he said to himself.

But the pain grew and spread to his entire body. Duke's vision began to blur, his head pounded. He tried to stand but fell to his knees. The bounty hunter's chest felt as if it was going to explode.

Or to have a heart attack.

His vision morphed from blurry to black in a matter of seconds. Duke felt as if he was a flat tire being filled with air...but a toxic air that burns you alive from the inside. He tried to open his eyes, but he couldn't see a thing. The pain increased as it spread over his body. He could feel himself slipping away, losing the fight to stay conscious.

Then it stopped.

He opened his eyes. He was staring down the lead ship. He blinked. At first rapidly, then slowly. The ship was still there, and he was still there. He looked down at his hands, they were still there. He looked down at his boots, they were still there. But they were now covering up the majority of the park. And Ol' Betsy looked like a discarded toothpick. Duke looked up again at the spacecraft and smiled. A *giant* smile.

CHAPTER 25

DUKE & THE FLEET

DUKE FELT A BARRAGE OF taps on his back. It felt as if an acupuncturist had lost control of their motor skills mid-session. They didn't hurt but they weren't exactly pleasant either. The now-gargantuan bounty hunter swung around and swatted at the pesky nuisances. Four of the five ships exploded on impact, the Jungafallowian Fighter spun out of control and retreated. The end of Duke's sleeve was now on fire. He shook it rapidly, but the flames would not go out. Two battle cruisers swooped in, lasers firing. These hurt a bit more than the mercenaries' ships but still nothing that would pierce his skin. He extended his hand to swat one of the cruisers, and the flames from his sleeve torched the craft instantaneously. It hurtled into the city center and exploded. The other ship peeled away, avoiding the makeshift blowtorch. He circled back but Duke caught it with his other hand. The battle cruiser kept firing. The Nova Texan simply pointed his new toy at the rest of the fleet, picking off a handful of the scout ships with the never-ending laser pulses.

This is starting to burn, realized Duke. He transferred

the battle cruiser into his other hand. It went up in flames immediately. His eyes surveyed the landscape beneath him.

"This should do it," he bellowed.

He plunged his burning arm into the park's brook, extinguishing the flames and turning the battle cruiser into an involuntary submarine. As he rose, smoke circling around his now frayed sleeve, he hurled the idle ship at a group of three battle cruisers that were repositioning for a probable attack. They all were destroyed.

This is kinda fun, he thought. *I could get used to this.*

The remaining battle cruiser and scout ships surrounded the lead spacecraft. They opened fire. This time, it hurt. A lot. Duke fell to his backside. The ships closed in, their firepower intensified. The bounty hunter made his way to a knee, but then the unknown ship opened fire. The energy beam lifted the bounty hunter off the ground and into a nondescript commercial complex, crushing a vintage clothing store and a diner. The fragrance of Irish whisky cake filled the air.

"That better not have been Aintin Kuniko's," shouted the bloodied giant.

Duke tried to stand up, but the attack was making it impossible. He tried to gain some stability with his right arm, and in the process his hand brushed up against his hip. More accurately, his holster. With his laser revolver. His *giant* laser revolver.

That thing grew too?

Instincts kicked in and Duke rattled off five pulses. The scout ships were obliterated. The battle cruiser was clipped significantly. It could not remain airborne and it skidded into a nearby field. The last pulse hit the lead ship, but it did not go down. It was damaged but not enough to halt its attack. However, without the other ships' weapons, Duke could withstand the energy beam for a while longer. He fired again, another direct hit. It spun the ship around, but it did not go down. It persisted. It was clearly a superior class of machine.

I wish I hadn't dropped Ol' Betsy, thought Duke.

The ship zoomed past Duke and circled back around, its beam connecting squarely with the bounty hunter's forearm. Duke fired back but missed. The ship began to employ evasive maneuvers, making it extremely difficult for Duke to hit. Even though he was an excellent marksman, especially with his laser revolver, he had never fired it as a skyscraper-dwarfing monster. It required some on-the-job recalibration. He fired again. Another miss. The ship closed the gap and landed a point-blank blast into the chest of the Nova Texan. Duke crashed to the Irish ground, flattening what remained of the park.

Duke's eyes opened and he could see the ship directly above him, approaching at breakneck speed with all weapons firing. At this point, the bounty hunter's entire body was in pain, the individual blasts weren't even distinguishable. Duke knew the heavily armed spacecraft was going in for the not-so-proverbial kill.

If I can take this pain for a bit longer, Duke thought to himself, *then I can do...this!*

The bounty hunter leapt up from his downed position and landed a quick pulse from his revolver to the tail end of the spacecraft. It tried to pull up but was hobbled. And in reach. Duke grabbed the spacecraft with both hands and drove it nose-first into the park ground.

"Mazilda," the giant bounty hunter stated, "I know you're in there. I know you're in this ship. And, most importantly, I know you're controlling these monsters. You better call them off or I will blast you right now."

He pointed his laser revolver at the immobile vessel.

"Turn those bastards off and surrender now. I'm waiting," continued Duke.

The banshee scream of the Winged Death was unmistakable. Visions of its rampage in Chicago filled Duke's head as soon as the screech pierced his ear canal. He turned to the west. Though it was on the other side of the city, he could make out a behemoth ninja scaling a cluster of buildings and leaping into the sky. He heard the screech again.

Ishiro'shea!

"See Mazilda, we have this under control," he said, turning back around.

But the ship was not there.

"Son of a—," Duke began before he caught the ship out of the corner of his eye. The craft was visibly damaged, wobbling aimlessly in the air. The bounty hunter regained his composure and aimed his laser revolver at the yo-yoing ship.

"Goodbye, Mazilda," he said softly to himself.

Before he could pull the trigger, his vision went blurry again. Then black. His body became crippled with pain. He was now a tire that was having its air sucked out in the most painful and excruciating manner. He collapsed.

When his eyes opened, he was looking up at the buildings that remained. He checked his hands, glanced down at his boots. They were there but now their normal sizes. He turned his head and saw Ol' Betsy. He looked up at the sky and the injured ship was gone.

CHAPTER 26

A WAR ROOM CHAT

THE WAR ROOM WAS A bit more subdued than it had been over the past few hours; admittedly, it's hard not to be when you are following an attempted kidnapping by an evil cyborg and slugfests with giant space monsters. At the table sat General Munger, Colonel Tott, the Father, Yumi, and the battered and bloodied crew of the *Deus Ex Machina*. At the very end, choosing to stand rather than sit, were Venksplin, Lantejira, and Sattlamora. A low-ranking soldier sprinted up behind the General, bent down, and whispered something in her ear. She nodded and the soldier scurried away silently.

"The Winged Death and the hobbled spacecraft have left Earth's atmosphere. The bug and the Aqua Demon haven't been located yet. We are scanning the waters around Ireland for the sea creature but the Underlord could prove difficult," Munger relayed to the table.

"Do you think they're dead?" asked the Father.

"No," replied Lilly and Po'l in unison.

"Don't get me wrong," continued the musk ox, "I'd like to think we gave them all they could handle but it's more likely that we did little more than give them a few bruises and hurt feelings. They are just taking a breather."

"So you think they will come back?" asked Colonel Tott.

"Without a doubt," Venksplin of the Yehaso said with a wince. "They are resilient creatures from what we have seen."

"Are you okay? You seem in pain," asked General Munger.

"As do you two," added Yumi, pointing to Sattlamora and Lantejira.

"We are fine," Venkplin answered. "The forceful abduction attempt by the Four I's might have made more of a physical impact on us than we originally thought. We apologize for the inconvenience."

"Not an inconvenience at all," responded the Father. "We just want to make sure that you're okay. I'm sure the adrenaline just delayed the pain."

Do they produce adrenaline? thought Duke.

General Munger cleared her throat, redirecting the attention back to her and the topics at hand.

"I don't know when, but like the Yehaso and our Gartoshian friend, I believe they will be back."

"And still controlled by Mazilda and that ship," cut in Duke.

"You don't know that, Duke," replied the Father. "You said yourself that it was just a hunch that the control mechanism was on the ship. Maybe it was on one of the others that you destroyed. And that's why the beasts are all heading away in different directions."

"I want to agree with you, but I know that ship had Mazilda on it. And I know she has some control. Somehow," responded Duke.

"With that being said, we appreciate the risk that all

four of you took with the potion. It was a valiant effort against those beasts. We might have learned how to combat them," proclaimed Munger. "The potion *did* work. I don't know how, it's beyond any of our scientific knowledge, but it did work. I think the clearest path to victory is to grow some of our top fighters to the size of the monsters and engage them in another round of combat."

Should I be insulted? Duke thought. *Yeah, I think I am insulted.*

"Your top fighters? You do realize that I won the Tournament of the Shield of the Colossal Calamari, right? None of your fighters would have made it through the first round. And Lilly, there, she is a Miss Bovine runner-up. Her only loss was to the Furry Mountain. *THE* Furry Mountain. Po'l fought against legions of evil priest warriors—not with long-range projectiles and lasers—but with his fists. And Ishiro'shea, well, he's leveled everyone from Sprinkles of the Trampling Death Robots to the death-dealer known as Tsarano Gar of Neprius. I don't think any of your trained baboons can do better than what we just did."

"I've never heard of any of those people," Tott interjected, his face as red as the blood of an Awlravian Jumping Cow. "Where the hell is Neprius anyways?"

"Calm down, Colonel," Munger said, placing her hand in front of the irate officer. "And Duke and crew, no offense was meant. I trust your fighting skills are as strong as any in our ranks. However, you are all nursing injuries from your battles. I can see them on your faces."

Duke looked around. Lilly sported a bandage around her shoulder from the acidic venom of the Underlord. Po'l sported a purple bruise across his cheek and his eye was almost completely shut. Even Ishiro'shea had seen better days; a bandage was wrapped around the majority of his torso and dried blood was still caked in clumps around his eyes. As Duke took in the scene, he started to feel his hand tingle from the intense burns from his own scuffle. Breathing became a bit more laborious. *Did Mazilda puncture a lung?* The bounty hunter began to understand where Munger was coming from.

"Fair point, General," he replied, nodding.

"And we know to hold on to our weapons," Yumi chirped. "It appears that if something is touching the subject that consumes the potion, it grows as well."

"So we should take it when sitting in a cube tank. Then we can blow them all to bits," shouted Tott in uncontrolled exuberance. "Blow. Them. All. Up. End of story."

Damn it, that makes a lot of sense, thought Duke. *Why did that testosterone-fueled blowhard have to say it?*

Venksplin leaned in over the shoulder of General Munger. All conversations halted; all eyes fixated on the Yehaso mouthpiece.

"We don't have any more potion," he said in an icy deadpan. "And we don't have the materials to make any more. We would need to return to Yehaso in order to gather the appropriate ingredients."

The energy that was building around a hopeful second round of giant-versus-monster combat bottomed out.

It was the hotheaded Colonel Tott who stood up. He looked around, making eye contact with everyone at the table.

"I'm out of ideas," he exclaimed. "Other than pelting them with more missiles and lasers and bombs, which has shown to do squat, I got nothing."

"I hate to agree with the Colonel but I'm in the same boat," replied Yumi.

General Munger's glance bounced from one person to the next, everyone shrugged their shoulders. No one had anything. It was a military writer's block of sorts.

"Okay then," Munger began. "I say we give it twenty-four hours. I will keep the defenses on full alert, but I think we have to start to consider a planet-wide evacuation."

"Wait, that's never been done. I don't think we can even do it," Tott shot back at his superior officer. "In theory—"

"Let's draw up the plans, Colonel," commanded the General. "I will begin to alert the Earth's top officials. The Father and Yumi can help. It will be a heavy undertaking, but I think we can clear the majority of the planet before these monsters destroy our world."

"We will need aid so that our transports aren't picked off by Four I's ships," recommended Yumi.

"Agreed," said Munger. "Can you reach back out to the Gartoshians and the Bounty Hunters Union? I know we're overdrawn on favors, but this will likely be the last—for obvious and unfortunate reasons."

The two military officials and Ishiro'shea's parents sped off from the war room to begin preparations.

"Twenty-four hours isn't very long to come up with a planet-saving plan," said Lilly.

"Nope, and let's call it twenty hours," responded Duke.

"Twenty?" inquired Po'l.

"Yep, because I need a drink. We all need a drink. Even you three need a drink," said Duke, nodding towards the pale-skinned alien trio.

"We don't have the same biological needs as your species," said Sattlamora. "We don't require the consumption of liquid at such high frequency intervals as humans or Gartoshians or primitive bipedal humanoids."

"Primitive—" began Po'l before Duke interjected.

"No, not drinks for survival—well not biological survival, at least—drinks for fun, washing away bad thoughts for a moment. Increasing joy. Just having a good ol' time. Those types of drinks."

"We are not familiar with those types of drinks," responded the bulky Lantejira.

"Buckle up, then. You are about to have a beverage or two with the fabled crew of the *Deus Ex Machina*," proclaimed Duke.

"Where do we meet this famous crew?" asked Sattlamora.

Duke covered his face with his hand and shook his head.

I'm going to need more than a few, he thought.

CHAPTER 27

WHAT CAN IT HURT, RIGHT?

THE BRIDGE OF THE *DEUS Ex Machina* had witnessed a drink or two in its day. So a small gathering of aliens from different sectors of the cosmos pouring a few glasses of alcohol as part of an impromptu happy hour was nothing out of the ordinary. The three Yehaso gathered around a raised cocktail table that sat in a corner of the bridge while Ishiro'shea, Lilly, and Po'l sat near the navigational panels, downing various forms of alcoholic beverages. Duke was the default bartender, or rather, the default waiter, ushering drinks to the guests—all the while, trying to imbibe his fair share of the mood-improving nectar. He approached the Yehaso with three glass bottles balanced carefully on the palm of his right hand and a mug of beer clutched in his left.

"What is this called again?" asked Venksplin in between groans.

"Glyptodian Summer Ale," answered Duke. "And are you okay?"

"Yes, why?" replied the Yehaso.

"You—matter of fact, all three of you, seem to be in some major pain. Hurting in a big way."

"The kidnapping," added Sattlamora. "It was the kidnapping that did this. More physical stress than we are accustomed to."

The bounty hunter pivoted and saw that the alien female was clutching her arm as if it was coming apart at the armpit.

"Right, the kidnapping," said Duke.

"Yes. I think we are getting better though," added Venksplin.

"And this will help," retorted Duke, holding up a frosted mug of ale. "I can't believe you've never had this stuff. It's kinda famous throughout most of the cosmos."

"Our race wasn't known for their deep space exploits and, though we have heard of alcohol from neighboring systems, the chemical compound does not exist as such on our planet," Venksplin continued.

"You've never had booze?" shouted Po'l, clearly overhearing the conversation from across the bridge. "Beer? Wine? Nothing?"

"I'm afraid not," replied the barrel-chested Lantejira.

"How did you—" Duke paused, searching for the right word, "—evolve?"

"I'm not sure I understand the question," said Lantejira.

"Life sucks, right? I mean, for the most part, you encounter some pretty undesirable crap in your lifetime. Would you agree?" asked Duke.

The frozen eyes of Lantejira returned a vacant stare.

"Right?" Duke asked again.

Now it was Sattlamora that possessed a confused gaze.

"Venksplin? My man. Surely, you've had some bad days, bad times," pressed the bounty hunter. "Before your planet was run over by the Cosmos, of course. Not every day was peachy, it couldn't have been."

The shortest Yehaso stroked his beard.

"Of course," Venksplin said bluntly. "There were always times of pain and grief. But what does that have to do with alcohol?"

Po'l, now standing right behind Duke, raised his glass of Erontian sake.

"Because this stuff helps with those bad times," he toasted. "And it tastes so good." He winked at Sattlamora but nothing was returned. Duke grinned.

"It hasn't been the best of times for us recently," began Venksplin as his focus narrowed on the three bottles of Glyptodian Summer Ale still balanced in Duke's hand.

"Things have not been going how they were designed," chimed in Sattlamora.

"Because of the kidnapping?" asked Duke.

There was no immediate response. But the bulky arm of Lantejira reached over and plucked one of the bottles from Duke's hand.

"Yes, the kidnapping," he grunted with a noticeable grimace.

Sattlamora followed suit, minus the growl. Venksplin was more measured but ended up grabbing the last bottle. Duke raised his mug.

"What can it hurt, right?" cheered the Nova Texan.

Venksplin nodded and took a quick sip of the ale. He stared down the cylindrical glass nozzle as if he was trying to find something floating in the golden pool. He looked up.

"This has a unique flavor. It is quite good, I think," Venksplin responded.

Sattlamora and Lantejira took their first drinks in unison. The resulting reaction was similar to Venksplin's.

"Y'all like it?" asked Duke.

"I think so," all three Yehaso harmonized.

Lilly, Po'l, Ishiro'shea, and Duke all raised their drinks in the air. The Yehaso followed suit.

"The good news is that we have a lot more where that came from," said Duke.

"One question," said Venksplin.

"Shoot," replied Duke.

"We still only have a few Earth hours to come up with a plan—" Venksplin began, before being cut off by the bounty hunter.

"No worries. I do my best thinking with a Glyptodian brew in my hand."

<hr>

There was a loud pounding echoing throughout the bridge of the *Deus Ex Machina*. Duke looked around; everyone was asleep. He peered into his most recently refilled mug of ale.

That went by pretty fast, he thought.

The pounding continued.

"I'm coming. Don't wake everyone up," he whispered to himself as he made his way to the elevator. He reached the bottom floor and shuffled to the door.

The rapping continued.

"Now you're really going to wake someone up," he said through the door. As he opened the entrance, he was surprised to see the scarlet-haired Private. Her skin was flushed, her eyes wide.

"General Munger wants to see you, uh, everyone," she said, rattling off the sentence as if it had been in her throat and trying to break free for ages. "They've spotted the Cosmoses."

"Mazilda?" asked Duke instinctually.

"I don't know but I don't think so. Just the three monsters," the Private replied.

"Everyone is asleep. I'll go," Duke replied. He stepped

out of the doorway but the Private didn't budge.

"The General wants everyone," she said, holding her ground.

"I have a sleeping Gartoshian musk ox, a drunk primitive warrior who, when startled, might tear off the head of a Mega-Troll, a ninja with a katana and a distrust in Earthers, and three aliens who just had their first sips of alcohol in their lives. By all means, go in there and wake them up," Duke replied, waving his hand towards the elevator door. "Be my guest."

"I—" the Private stammered.

"Yes, I know. The General is going to be disappointed," interrupted Duke. "I'll take the heat on this one, kid. I'll tell her that I'm the only one in the *Deus*. If she doesn't believe me, then I'll think of another lie."

The soldier simply stepped to the side and let Duke pass by.

It was a pretty short walk from the landing strip to the war room. Outside of a few guards who looked about as "on guard" as his drunk compatriots back on the *Deus*, it was extremely quiet. Even when he entered the war room, there were only a handful of military personnel scuttling about and only a fraction of the monitors were turned on. But the General was there. Next to her were Colonel Tott, the Father, and Yumi. All four had their arms folded and were staring intensely at a grouping of three screens.

"What can I do you for?" asked Duke, raising his half-full mug of Glytpodian Summer Ale.

"Where is everyone?" asked the General.

"Where are the Yehaso?" added Tott.

Duke shrugged his shoulders. "I'm not their babysitter. We had a few drinks. After that, who knows."

Tott's face flashed a bright red. Duke could feel the heat pumping out from the angry Colonel's skin.

"Seriously, what's going on? You guys cook up a plan?" asked Duke.

"Not a plan, as such," said the Father. "But something interesting. Maybe a really positive finding."

"And that would be?" asked Duke.

The four parted to reveal the three screens.

On the first, wedged up alongside a rocky shoreline of what appeared to be an island, was the Aqua Demon. He wasn't moving. In the middle screen was the Underlord, half submerged in an open field. Idle. On the last screen was a clearing at the top of a plateau. Duke wasn't familiar enough with Earth geography to know where it was but in the middle of it, collapsed on its side, was the Winged Death.

"Are they dead?" he asked cautiously.

"We don't think so," replied General Munger. "But it appears that their skirmishes with your friends did more damage than we imagined. It appears that they need time to recharge. This could be our moment to attack. The opening that we need."

"Okay, maybe I should have woken them up. They would've wanted to see this," said Duke.

"Who? I thought you said you didn't know where they were," fired back Tott.

"Oh yeah, never mind. Just talking to myself," Duke replied. *Must change subject.* "So, General Munger, what's the plan? What are you going to do?"

"I wanted to ask the Yehaso if they had any ideas before we commit to an attack. And before they wake up," she replied.

"We might be too late," said the Father. "That one is stirring."

The Winged Death was fluttering its wings. It pressed up with its arms until its hind legs were under it. Then the forelegs. It rose up quickly but then shuffled to the right, lost its balance, and collapsed again.

"It's still hurt," barked Tott. "Let's move on this now, General."

"I agree," the General responded. "Call it in."

"Duke, try and round up the rest of the crew, wherever they are?" asked Yumi. "We need everyone here. This could be our only chance."

Duke tipped his hat and headed back to the *Deus*.

He paused a few paces short of the opening that led to the landing strip where his ship—and his passed-out comrades—rested comfortably.

Wait a second. I don't think that monster was hurt.

CHAPTER 28

TEST DESIGN

OF ALL OF THE PARTICIPANTS in their extended happy hour, Ishiro'shea and Duke were the only ones that seemed mildly functional. Hell, Duke never even fell asleep. And he was headache-free, at the moment. Po'l and Lilly entered the war room, eyes squinting, and their individual gaits had a bit more sway than normal. The Yehaso shuffled in behind them. They did not look well. But their pains seemed to be more from the booze than their previous injuries sustained from the attempted kidnapping by Mazilda's friendly cyborg.

"How's it going, my alien friends?" Duke said with a smile. "Enjoy the Glyptodian ale?"

The Yehaso did not respond. They were really laboring as they inched into the war room, huddled together as a single entity.

Guess not, concluded Duke.

"Explain again why you woke us up and brought us here? New information or something?" asked Lilly.

"Actually, I asked to bring you here," chimed in General Munger. "I thought you'd want to see this." She pointed to the triumvirate of monitors.

It was the Winged Death, the Underlord, and the Aqua Demon. All in the exact same places as a few moments before. They were rustling around but they still looked injured.

"I knew we hurt those bastards," moaned Po'l, closing his eyes as if simply speaking was a form of physical torture.

"It appears so," said Munger. "It appears that they are injured, and this could be our last chance to strike. That's why I wanted the Yehaso here." She turned to face the alien trio. "Is there anything you recommend? If we have one shot at this, I want to have as much information before we call in an attack. Thoughts?"

The Yehaso did not respond right away. They all slowly lifted their heads in unison.

"I'm sorry, General," Venksplin began, "could you repeat what you just said? But maybe a bit softer?"

"What's wrong with you?" snapped Colonel Tott. "You look hungover."

"Yeah, they might be. Or maybe still a bit drunk. I'm not an expert on Yehaso biology," said Duke, grinning. "We had a few drinks to celebrate or contemplate or something like that."

The blood vessels in Tott's eyes exploded. He flared his teeth at the bounty hunter as if he was some unevolved werebeast.

The Father stepped in front of Tott before he could advance on Duke.

"Duke, that was probably not the best idea," the Father said in a stern paternal tone. "With such a limited window in which the fate of our planet hinges, a party probably wasn't the appropriate course of action."

"It wasn't much of a party," Po'l added. "The Yehaso aren't much fun, if you ask me."

"Shut up, Po'l," snapped Lilly, covering his mouth with her mammoth hand.

"Regardless," General Munger interjected, "I am curious as to what the Yehaso say." She lowered her voice and repeated the question. "We have one shot at this, is there anything in particular that you recommend for our attack on the injured Cosmoses?"

The Yehaso turned away from the General and huddled together. Duke tried to eavesdrop, but he couldn't make out anything other than faint mumbling. The secretive chat went on for a few minutes before they all redirected their attention to the General.

"We have revisited every piece of information that we know. Revisited every theory that our people had on the Cosmoses. But we need some more time. We will return to our quarters and analyze the situation," proclaimed Venksplin.

Though Colonel Tott had the market cornered on hotheadedness, General Munger made sure to show off her ability to be outraged. Though it was done with a tad more restraint and decorum. But it was just as scary.

"We don't have time," she said through gritted teeth. Her temples were pulsating. "This is our last opportunity. Do you have a recommendation?"

The Yehaso seemed unfazed by the General's obvious frustration.

Can they just not read people yet? Or are they still drunk? pondered Duke.

"We need time to review the situation," said Sattlamora.

"Fine, we will do it ourselves," exclaimed General Munger. She turned back around and began to bark orders at the few soldiers in the war room. Tott followed behind her.

Good boy, good little Tott, chuckled Duke to himself.

The Father and Yumi approached the Yehaso, attempting to plead the severity of the situation and rationalize with the mopey aliens.

Duke grabbed Ishiro'shea's shoulder.

"Hey bud, you aren't going to like what I'm about to do. It won't make sense. But trust me. I'll explain later," he whispered to his ninja companion.

Ishiro'shea shook his head.

"Trust me," Duke repeated.

The ninja threw his arms in the air and turned around.

Brace for impact, Duke said to himself.

The bounty hunter motioned to Lilly and Po'l. The two made their way over, with a slight zig and slightly more zag.

He put his arm around Po'l and leaned in. Lilly did the same. Ishiro'shea stood nearby but didn't participate in the woozy huddle.

"Hey, I didn't want to cause a problem or stir the pot," Duke began softly, "but the big Yehaso guy, uh, Lantejira, was telling his buddies last night that the Aqua Demon was beating you down, Po'l. He said that you shrunk down and ran away, tail between your legs."

Po'l's half-opened eyes ballooned up into orbs of fire. A half-drunk, half-hungover rage was as irrational as any rage —and with less inhibitions. A perfect combination for Duke's theory.

"That son of a—" began Lilly, but Po'l had already left the semicircle.

Ishiro'shea flashed a glance of disapproval at Duke.

"Hold on. Trust me," mouthed Duke to his sidekick. Ishiro did not release his stare.

Po'l rushed headlong towards the Yehaso. He clipped the Father with his shoulder, pushing him and Yumi out of the way. He got so close to Lantejira that their noses touched each other, or rather Po'l's nose touched the chin of the larger alien.

"What did you say about me and the giant lizard?" Po'l shouted. "You said I couldn't take it. You said I was getting beat, huh?"

Lantejira did not waver. He did not flinch or change his expression.

"How about you say it to my face, big guy?" continued Po'l.

"Stop it," cried Yumi. "This is no time for this behavior."

"C'mon, big fella, don't back down," Duke whispered to himself.

The bounty hunter's arm felt like it was in a vice grip. He turned around and saw Ishiro'shea, his eyes blazing hot.

Before the ninja could say anything, Duke motioned for him to calm down.

This plan better work or Ish is going to kill me, thought Duke.

Po'l continued to berate the Yehaso. Sattlamora and Venksplin had stepped away from the standoff but the Father and Yumi did not disengage. Finally, it was Yumi who peeled Po'l away from Lantejira.

Damn, thought Duke.

"Okay, Ish, it seems like my idea didn't—" started Duke.

As Yumi pushed Po'l away from Lantejira, the behemoth Yehaso landed a right hand to the face of the Neprian. Po'l flew in the air and hit the ground with a thud. The Father rushed in between his wife and Lantejira. The Yehaso looked back at the other two and flashed a quick smile.

"Wait for it," Duke said to Ishiro'shea.

Before Lantejira could turn back to face his downed opponent, he was on the floor with a former Miss Bovine runner-up standing over him, fists clenched.

The war room erupted at the sight of the knocked out Yehaso. Screaming. Yelling. Accusations. Sheer pandemonium.

Duke grabbed Ishiro'shea and positioned him away from the confusion.

"Look at the screen, Ish," instructed Duke. "Look at the Aqua Demon, in particular. It was waddling around, regaining its composure, and look at it now."

The ninja stared at the screen. Then back at his long-time friend. Then at Lantejira on the floor.

"See?" said the bounty hunter.

Ishiro'shea returned his gaze to the Aqua Demon.

The massive sea monster was on its back, motionless.

CHAPTER 29

VOILA

"WE SHOULD PROBABLY STAY IN here for a bit, while things cool down," said Duke, extending his legs onto the railing around his captain's chair. "And they sorta ordered us to do so...so there's that."

"Sounds good to me," Po'l responded, an ice pack over his left eye. "Can't believe I was sucker punched by that piece of garbage. I'm going to get him back before we leave this planet."

Duke chuckled. "I think Lilly took care of that for you, buddy."

"Oh yeah," Po'l said with a grin. "Thanks for that, Lil. I wish I could've seen it."

Lilly patted Po'l on the head and began to recount the episode before the lovefest was interrupted by a series of pointed grunts. Ishiro'shea motioned to Duke. Po'l and Lilly turned to face the bounty hunter.

"Oh, right. I should probably come clean, huh, Ish?" Duke said. He stood up. "First off, I'm sorry, Po'l. I totally used you."

"What are you talking about?" asked the Neprian.

"Lantejira never said those things about you," Duke

confessed. "I lied to you to see if you'd get in a scuffle with him."

"Were *you* too scared?" Po'l responded. He leapt up to his feet, dropping his ice pack on the floor. "You better have a good reason, LaGrange."

"Yeah, it better be really good," added Lilly, her hands on her hips. "I don't like knocking out people under false pretenses, you know."

"Calm down. It's a really, *really* good reason. If it wasn't, don't you think Ishiro'shea would've called me out by now?" Duke replied.

"So spill it," Lilly demanded.

"I realized I was wrong about Mazilda," Duke began.

"We are aware of that, genius," smirked Po'l.

Duke ignored the comment and continued. "I was wrong about Mazilda and her ship controlling the space monsters. I don't think she or her ship could control them."

"But they were clearly working in tandem," interjected Lilly.

"Agreed. When we were drinking up here last night, that very thought kept me up. How was this happening? Did someone in her force train them? Brain control? Were they giant mechs made to look like biological entities to throw people off? I was stumped. But then when I—well, we—were summoned by Munger to go and check out the new footage of the Cosmoses, it hit me."

"This is the time when we were all asleep?" asked Lilly.

"Yep," replied Duke. "All three of those bastards were out cold."

"Injured from our battles," said Po'l.

"Maybe. But maybe not," replied the bounty hunter. "Yes, you did do some damage. But not enough that they were all virtually unconscious."

"Sleeping?" asked Lilly.

"I think I would have come to that conclusion too had I not seen what happened next," said Duke. "The flying one started to stand up but lost its balance, shuffled around a bit, and collapsed. Just like it was—"

"Drunk," stated Lilly, finishing his sentence.

"Just like the Yehaso," proclaimed Duke. He sat back down in his captain's chair. "So, what I'm saying is that the Yehaso are controlling the monsters. Not Mazilda. Not the Four I's. The saviors of Earth aren't really saviors."

The bridge on the *Deus* was quiet.

"You've lost your ever-loving mind, LaGrange," said Po'l, breaking the silence. "Why would they do it?"

" I don't know," said Duke bluntly.

"How?" asked Po'l.

"I don't know," he repeated.

"Why Earth?" Po'l asked.

"I don't know," said Duke.

"Do you know anything? This is a pretty big claim, even for you. What do you think, Lilly?" asked Po'l.

She snorted and walked toward the forward screen of the *Deus*.

"Can you explain the episode with Po'l, then?" she bellowed.

"By all means," Duke began. "When everyone was in the war room, all three monsters were up and about, albeit on the woozy side. Like the Yehaso were at that moment. But they were up, that's the main takeaway. I needed to find a way to render one of them 'not up' without raising too many suspicions from Munger or Tott or the Yehaso. No one would think twice about a drunk primitive trying to pick a fight when his manhood has been challenged. And that's where Po'l came in. Of the three, I had a feeling Lantejira would be the most likely Yehaso to engage with you, especially in their state. Call it a hunch. Then, voila."

"And when I knocked out Lantejira—" Lilly started.

"The sea serpent collapsed. Out cold," Po'l said, finishing her thought. "Is this even possible?"

"I've heard of certain species that share symbiotic links with other life-forms—like the Monster Riders of Raya-Hon," said Lilly. "But symbiotic links and telepathic communication are a far cry from actually controlling another species. And, if your theory holds, Duke, this is a strong connection."

"Exactly," said Duke. "The question is, what now? There's no way Munger or Tott will believe this. No chance at all."

Lilly leaned against the circular railing. Po'l sat back down, his ice pack back on his bruised eye, and Ishiro'shea sat, legs crossed, on the floor.

"On top of the 'what now,' we probably need to understand the 'why,'" said Lilly. "There has to be a motive."

"I have a plan," shouted Po'l.

"You do?" inquired Duke.

"I do. And don't sound so shocked, ass," Po'l replied. "You still have that sleep serum in here?"

"Yeah. I think I see where you're heading with this, Po'l. Sneaky," replied Duke.

"Maybe it's time that I go apologize for my earlier actions," the Neprian said, smiling.

CHAPTER 30

AN APOLOGY

"I STILL CAN'T BELIEVE THAT you all got into a fight with the only three beings in the universe who might be able to save us," said Yumi Nobunaga-Flaherty on the main view screen of the *Deus Ex Machina*. "I mean, we could be minutes away from our planet being destroyed and you lot are getting into a drunken squabble about who is tougher than whom."

"We know," said Duke with a slight bow. "And we're sorry. And that's why we want to apologize to the Yehaso in person. If anything, to show them that we are appreciating all that they're doing to help Earth. I will take blame for providing the booze. Po'l, for attacking Lantejira regarding his comments. And Lilly, well, for sucker punching the Yehaso."

Duke didn't need to look back to know that Lilly was fuming inside at the notion that she sucker punched anyone. But it was for the good of the cause, in this case.

"It's not up to us, unfortunately. It's up to General Munger. Let us go talk to her and see what we can do," replied the Father.

"It will be in the interest of planetary security. We need the Yehaso fully engaged," added Duke.

The screen cut out.

"Now we wait. Anyone want a drink?"

The door opened and an armed contingent of eight soldiers were there to meet the four space travelers. They all raised their hands as they left the ship.

"You're not under arrest," smirked one of the soldiers. "We just want to make sure you don't try any funny business."

"Fair enough. I guess it's habit when people point laser rifles at us," replied the bounty hunter.

The soldier ordered the rest of the squad to lower their weapons. "This way," he growled.

After traversing the corridors of the base, including the roofless portion from the attempted kidnapping, they approached the Yehaso's quarters.

"They know we're coming but I'm going to knock regardless," muttered the lead soldier.

"Sensible," replied Lilly.

"And courteous," added Duke.

The soldier ignored their comments and rapped on the Yehaso's door three times. After a momentary delay, Venksplin peeked his head out. His eyes met Duke's and he slid back inside the room. After some murmuring, all three Yehaso appeared. Lantejira in the front and Venksplin and Sattlamora flanking him.

"Okay, they're here," said the lead soldier. "Say your piece. Do your thing. Just hurry it up. I'm not sure how long those monsters are going to stay down."

Duke stepped forward first. Ishiro'shea was at his side.

"First, I want to apologize for forcing your hands into drinking our potent alcohol. I should have been more forthcoming with information about its effects on certain lifeforms. I prevented you from making an informed decision. For that, I am truly sorry."

The bounty hunter and his ninja sidekick bowed in tandem, then stepped to the side, allowing the lumbering Gartoshian musk ox to step forward.

"Lantejira, I apologize with all of my being for the cheap shot that I took. I was not in the right mindset from the alcohol and acted as a poor representative of my race and this unified front to defend Earth," she said, bowing at the end.

"Thank you," replied Lantejira. "I have met other Gartoshians during our Earthbound endeavors and I find your race respectful and honest. May you continue to follow in their image."

Lilly bowed again before giving way for Po'l.

"My Yehaso friends, I am the one who owes you the biggest apology," began Po'l. "If anyone understands your plight, it's me. I am the only one of my race here; and though my people do exist, they are contained in such a unique corner of space that only strange magical cosmic anomalies can get you there. In essence, I am the lone survivor of the Neprian people. Like Lilly, the drink made me act like a hooligan. A *primitive*. I falsely accused you, Lantejira. I am ashamed of my actions and please, I beg you, don't take out your frustrations with us—with me—on the good people of Earth. They need you."

Po'l finished with the deepest bow of the group. He held it there for some time.

Venksplin rotated in front of Lantejira. He returned the bow.

"We thank you for owning up to your mistakes, fellow

space travelers and defenders of Earth," he began, before Po'l cut him off.

"Oh, one more thing. On my home planet, we embrace to solidify the act of forgiveness," the Neprian proclaimed. "So come here!"

It was clear that all three Yehaso were trying to object to the foreign notion of a hug, but Po'l was on a mission. He didn't give them a chance to verbalize their hesitations. His arms were squeezing Venksplin so tight that the alien's eyes began to bulge. From the look on the Yehaso's face, he was not enjoying this "Neprian custom." Po'l launched himself at Lantejira, wrapping the brawny Yehaso in a tight bear hug. Lantejira seemed as uncomfortable as Venksplin. Po'l approached Sattlamora. Her face, somehow, was even whiter than was typical.

"Don't be scared. You're my favorite of the lot," he said with a phony smile. "Come here!"

He's committed, I'll give him that, thought Duke. *A bit creepy, but committed.*

Po'l hugged Sattlamora, lifted her in the air briefly, and set her back down.

"I don't care much for these embraces that are part of your native customs, Neprian," she said as her feet hit the floor. "They aren't very pleasant. They hurt even."

The Neprian turned to face his comrades. He winked.

"I think we should all go up to tell the General that we've made up and everything is just fine and dandy," began Duke. "Don't you?"

The guards did not answer and began shuffling the crew of the *Deus Ex Machina* back down the hallway.

"Our orders were to watch you apologize and get you back to your ship. You're still under house arrest," the lead soldier barked.

"See, I told you it was like being arrested," quipped Duke.

Po'l tapped Duke on the shoulder as they walked down the long corridor.

"Not good, guys," he said, his voice quivering. He showed Duke the syringe. But there wasn't a needle.

The sound of the body hitting the floor permeated throughout the hallway. The guards looked back and saw Sattlamora collapsed on the floor. Four of the eight rushed back. They knelt down and examined the body.

"This isn't good," Duke whispered. "Right about now they should be finding the—"

One of the soldiers attending to the downed Yehaso lifted up a needle. It twinkled in the artificial illumination of the corridor.

"—needle," finished Duke.

The bounty hunter and his friends turned around and were staring directly into the ends of four laser rifles. He heard the lead soldier say, "Send backups. Duke and his crew tried to kill one of the Yehaso."

"We surrender," shouted Duke, arms raised in the air. "We surrender. Just take us to General Munger and Colonel Tott in the war room. We will explain everything."

A dozen more armed guards filed in from both ends of the corridor.

CHAPTER 31

ARRESTED

"HOW IS THE YEHASO FEMALE?" asked Munger from the head of the table. She was surrounded by Colonel Tott, Father Flaherty, Yumi, and Venksplin. Next to them were some other military officials. Yeop stood in the back against the wall. Duke tried not to make eye contact with their friend; if disappointment could ever be summed up in a single expression, it was on Yeop's face at that very moment.

Duke, Ishiro'shea, Lilly, and Po'l were on the opposite end of the table. Their weapons removed. And four laser rifles pointed directly at the backs of their heads. Somewhere behind them was Lantejira. Duke could feel his presence.

"She is resting in our quarters," answered Venksplin. "Thank you for the additional security detail outside of our room. It is much appreciated."

"It's the least that we could do," replied Munger.

Duke glanced over at Yumi. She was crying. Her son, the one she just got back, was being held captive by her own planet's military.

I really hope this works, thought Duke. *Or Ishiro'shea is going to kill me, if these Earthers don't first.*

"I don't even know where to begin," said Munger. "Do you have anything to say?"

"Why thank you for the opportunity," Duke said. His jovial attitude clearly caught the military personnel off guard. "The 'why' will become very clear if you simply flip on the monitor to whatever channel is picking up the sleeping centaur Cosmos thingy. Just pop that on and you'll see everything."

"What?" asked Tott.

"Just do it, Colonel," said Munger, her eyes not leaving the bounty hunter's. "Let's see what LaGrange is talking about."

"Thank you," Duke said with a head nod.

The monitor flickered and then the feed stabilized. Clear as day was the Winged Death. It was on the very same plateau that Duke had originally seen it stumble and bumble around in a drunken stupor. But the mighty space centaur was asleep.

"Voila," Duke said, waving his hands as if he completed a magic trick.

Duke scanned the attendees.

No one is getting it, he realized.

"Do you not see it?" the Nova Texan asked.

"What? The sleeping Cosmos?" asked Munger.

"Exactly!" exclaimed Duke. "It proves everything. It proves what these Yehaso really are."

Side conversations sprung up around the table.

"No time for riddles, LaGrange," replied Munger. "What are you trying to say?"

Duke took a deep breath. "Sattlamora is out cold, thanks to our sleep serum. Zonked out. And guess who else is—the Winged Death. When Lantejira got knocked out—also orchestrated by yours truly—guess who else was knocked out? The Aqua Demon. Mazilda and the Four I's aren't controlling these monsters. The Yehaso are."

"Preposterous," shouted Venksplin. It was the first time that Duke had heard one of the Yehaso raise their voices. "You attack us. You drug us. And we're the wrongdoers?"

"This is insane, even for a nut like you," Tott smirked. "Just throw them in jail and let's get this attack ordered."

The side conversations escalated. Murmurs became giggles, giggles became laughter.

"You're losing them," Lilly said to Duke.

"How are they not putting two and two together?" he asked the Gartoshian.

But Duke noticed the Father and Yumi. They weren't part of any of the side conversations. They were talking to General Munger. As Tott led the peanut gallery in a good laugh, Munger seemed to be seriously considering the claim. Duke noticed that Venksplin was also paying close attention to the general.

"General!" Duke yelled over the background noise. "I can prove it to you. I mean, I can prove it to you *more*."

The general's face was emotionless.

"And how is that?" she asked.

"I'd rather not yell it, if it's all the same. It will give it away and prevent the truth from being exposed. Can I please approach you three?" he asked.

"Absolutely not!" screamed Tott. "Don't be crazy!"

"Colonel, I'm fine with it," Munger replied.

"But General—"

"I'm fine with it. Drop it," the General commanded. Tott disappeared back into the crowd of disbelieving soldiers poking fun at the bounty hunter's hypothesis.

Duke raised his hands and slowly stood up. As he made his way over to the General, the Father, and Yumi—with two soldiers' laser rifles pointed at the back of his head—he made sure to take the route closest to Venksplin. As he passed the Yehaso, Duke gave him a wink. Venksplin did not reciprocate.

He has no idea as to what's about to happen, Duke thought.

Duke could feel the barrel of both guns just behind each ear. He stopped his walk mid-step, the gun barrels grazed the brim of his hat. Before the low-ranking soldiers could react, Duke had grabbed both guns and dislodged them from the soldiers' grasps. He tossed them across the room. The last thing he wanted to do was to have someone think he was trying to kill anyone. Duke knew he had only a second or two before he was overtaken by the other guards, so he didn't want to waste it. He clenched his right fist and extended it with force directly into the nose of Venksplin. The Yehaso crumbled to the floor. As soon as he fell, a swarm of soldiers engulfed the Nova Texan.

"Look at the monitor! Look at the bug!" Duke shouted from the bottom of the pile.

All the bounty hunter could see was black.

When the bodies started to peel off of Duke and the light of the war room became visible, the first face he saw was that of the Father. He reached down and extended a hand to Duke. He yanked up and propelled Duke to his feet.

That is one strong priest, thought Duke.

Yumi walked over to her husband and embraced him. General Munger was looking the bounty hunter up and down. Her face was still devoid of any tells, of any emotion. After a heartbeat, she turned her head towards the monitor. The Winged Death was still out. The screen next to it now showcased the giant cosmic beetle. It wasn't moving. Stone cold knocked out.

Munger took in a deep breath. "Release Duke and his crew. Wake up Venksplin. He needs to explain himself."

"He's not here," said a soldier. "He *was* here. But he's gone."

"Did no one have eyes on him?" Munger asked.

"In the commotion—" pleaded another soldier.

"Lantejira's gone too," shouted Lilly.

"Get them!" commanded Munger. "Now!"

CHAPTER 32

LOGIC

T HE YEHASO'S QUARTERS WERE IMPECCABLY clean. If they had rushed back, gathered a few things, and hit the road in a hurry, it was hard to tell. Duke opened drawers and peered in closets. Empty.

"You think they're hiding in their dresser?" asked Lilly. "Seems unlikely, given the laws of space and—"

"Weren't you like five hundred feet tall a few hours ago?" jabbed Duke.

"Fair point, cowboy," the musk ox replied with a smirk.

"And I was looking for any clues. Anything they left behind that might give us an idea. I mean, this base isn't *that* big."

"And we haven't registered any stolen ships leaving or visitors touching down. They have to be *here*," added the Father. "Maybe Ishiro'shea and Po'l are having better luck near the hangar."

Duke did not reply. He kept searching for something. Anything.

"And Duke," the Father continued, "I am sorry for how this all went down. We should have trusted you."

"It's okay. I know my approach was unconventional.

But unconventional situations sometimes call for it. I'm just glad we know who's on our side and who's on Mazilda's side," Duke replied.

"So do you think if we stop the Yehaso, we stop the monsters?" asked the Irishman.

"If by 'stop' you mean 'kill,' then yes. I could be wrong. But when they were drunk, the monsters were drunk. When they were knocked out, the monsters were knocked out. Logic dictates that if we kill them, they should die too," Duke rationalized.

"But weren't you a skyscraper-sized giant a few hours ago?" retorted Lilly. "Are we using logic now, LaGrange?"

"Fair point," replied Duke.

They continued to search the room—then the neighboring rooms—and found nothing. It was like the Yehaso never spent a single night at the Earth base.

Duke, Lilly, and the Father were about to head back to the war room to report their lack of findings when Po'l and Ishiro'shea came into view. Both men were sprinting down the hall toward the trio. They stopped a nose length's from the group.

"Hey, we were trying to find you," said Po'l, struggling to catch his breath. "Just saw Munger and Tott. No sign of the Yehaso but the monsters are on the move."

"That means Sattlamora and Venksplin are probably awake. And now that *they* know *we* know, they will waste no time in attacking," said Duke.

"And it will allow them to get away since we'll focus on the impending monster invasion," added the Father.

"But that's where they're wrong," said Duke. "Yes, the monsters are probably going to do a ton of damage, but the only way we're going to stop them is to find the Yehaso and take their pale asses out. If they are hiding and are going to make a run for it, it will be now when eyes will be diverted."

"I'll be the eyes," said the Father. "I'll head back to the control room and make sure scanners are tight on the perimeter, even if we are going to be blown to bits by one of the Cosmoses. I'll relay if we see anything. Sound good?"

"Perfect," said Duke with a nod. "Thank you."

Before Duke could tip his hat, the Father had disappeared down a corridor.

"I guess we split up. Keep comms open. Each of us take an exit," commanded Duke.

"Aren't there like thirty exits in this compound?" asked Po'l.

All four looked at each. The realization that their odds of picking the right escape route weren't great, and that's assuming the Yehaso would actually try to escape as Duke had theorized.

"Well, just pick the right one then," said Duke.

***

Duke knelt down behind some scrap machinery that stood just outside one of the back exits to the base. It led down an alleyway deep into the heart of New Tokyo. In the distance, he could see a fenced-off clearing. There was no exit visible to the bounty hunter.

Probably not the ideal escape route, considering it's a dead end, surmised Duke. *I guess I'll try another.*

Duke stood up and headed back inside the base; as he made his way through the threshold of the ajar door, an earsplitting wail echoed throughout the alleyway. It was followed by the simultaneous explosion of every glass window in the vicinity.

The Winged Death.

The bounty hunter lunged inside to prevent being pelted by the rainfall of broken glass. The entire alleyway and subsequent open lot were pocked with shards from thousands of high-rise windows. The wail came again. Duke peeked out from behind the open door and gazed toward the sky. Sure enough, the massive space centaur was hovering over the skyline of New Tokyo. The flying Cosmos whipped his head and disseminated a laser from his single eye. It whizzed across the rows of buildings and struck the base. The building rocked and swayed. Duke lost his balance and tumbled out into the alleyway, behind the same mound of unused machine parts that he was behind moments ago. The bounty hunter tried to stand but hit the ground again as a melting heat permeated from above. An intense spread of fire consumed the air. Though he was multiple stories below the behemoth flames, he could feel his flesh burning.

The Aqua Demon.

"That means the—" Duke began to himself before being thrown off his balance again.

The ground rumbled. The pile of machine parts toppled over. Debris began to fall from the tops of surrounding buildings. He heard a loud shriek that couldn't have been more than a few blocks away.

"—Underlord," Duke said finishing his sentence.

Still on the ground, Duke brushed away some of the glass that clung to his pants and grabbed his communicator.

"Ishiro, Lilly, Po'l, anyone? Any luck with the Yehaso? It seems that the Cosmoses have all converged on the base," Duke yelled as debris continued to rain down from above.

"Nothing," replied Lilly.

"Nothing here either," answered Po'l.

Another ball of fire appeared overhead, courtesy of the Aqua Demon. Duke instinctually hit the ground and covered up. He felt some of the glass shards digging into his skin.

"We better find them soon," said Lilly, "because this town isn't surviving much longer."

"We aren't surviving either," added Po'l. "If we are supposed to wait outside for these aliens, there are pretty good odds that I get squashed by one of the buildings."

The Winged Death let loose another potent laser strike, disintegrating a nearby building.

"Let's abort," shouted Duke. "I was wrong. They aren't trying to escape. At least not during this firestorm."

Duke had made it to his hands and knees when he saw three icy-white figures dart from an open door and into the alley. Lantejira led the way with both Sattlamora and Venksplin trailing after. They had both made a seemingly remarkable recovery from a sleeping serum and a patented right jab from Duke LaGrange. Duke's ego was a little bruised by Venksplin's recovery time.

They sprinted down the alley into the clearing. Duke followed them but made sure not to make his presence known.

Little do they know that they're heading right into a dead end, thought Duke. *It'll be like shooting fish in a barrel.*

They made a hard left. And there it was. It was a dead end, yes, but dead ends tend to be less dead endy when there's a shuttle craft waiting for you.

Shit.

The Yehaso scurried inside the boxy craft. It would have been hard-pressed to fit more than five beings inside of it; however, its limited size gave it the much needed ability to hide itself in an insignificant alleyway mere steps from the Earth's most important military base without detection. The ship was already ten feet off the ground when Duke snapped to and racked his brains for what to do next.

The ship began to dart away from the monster-created

destruction when Duke hoisted Ol' Betsy in the air. He zeroed in on the craft and fired.

Despite three space monsters destroying the city around him with metal-melting acid, piercing laser beams, and fireballs the size of asteroids, Betsy's song was not to be muffled. It was as loud as ever, outpacing the decibel levels of all of the Cosmoses' most damaging offensive tactics.

The right side of the fleeing escape craft ignited. Betsy had made her presence known. Unfortunately, it was not a direct hit. The ship wobbled, struggling to right itself and fly straight. The damage was substantial. It started to descend on a flattened trajectory. The shuttle was out of Duke's sights as it approached an unplanned landing somewhere in New Tokyo's decimated industrial district.

CHAPTER 33

FLIPPER PRINTS AREN'T GOOD HIDING SPOTS

THE THREE COSMOSES WERE ALL stomping New Tokyo into oblivion. Few buildings remained upright, and those that did were shells of their former towering glories. Every screen in the war room was broadcasting the demolition, and it was clear that every person in the war room was in a panic.

"Any sign of the damaged Yehaso ship?" Duke asked over Tott's shoulder as the Colonel was peering into a screen on the table. "I know I hit it and it couldn't have gone far. Check the industrial—"

"Can't you see we're dealing with something a bit bigger than those three aliens?" interrupted Tott. "Your hare-brained theories will have to be discussed at another time; right now, I have to try and take down three giant space monsters who are hell-bent on wiping this city from the face of the Earth. Oh, and weren't you guarding the door that they escaped out of?"

Duke sighed.

What a short-sighted twit, he thought.

The bounty hunter approached General Munger. Her dark skin was almost without color at the moment. *Panic doesn't do justice to what she must be going through*, thought Duke. Her eyes darted from tactical screen to tactical screen. She gave orders to approaching soldiers without even making eye contact as if she just sensed their presence. Duke was no different.

"No time, LaGrange," she said, her gaze fixated on a readout from one of the tabletop screens.

"General, the Yehaso—" he pleaded.

"The Yehaso are gone, LaGrange. We have to try and salvage what's left of New Tokyo before it's too late," the general replied. "I encourage you to do whatever you can to help that cause."

Munger continued on but Duke had already walked away. He signaled for Lilly, Po'l, and Ishiro'shea to join him outside in the hallway. When all four were gathered around, Duke began to speak.

"Munger, Tott, and the rest in here can't see the forest for the trees. They're lasering in on these monsters when they should be trying to track down that ship with the Yehaso," Duke began.

"You don't think that Mazilda hasn't already picked them up?" asked Lilly. "She sent a ship down for them, so you know she's tracking it. She probably had an extraction team at the ready."

"Possibly, but we have to hope they're still out there," said Duke. "I say we hop in the *Deus* and try and track down those bastards. And we have a better chance at killing some Four I's out there than we do in here."

The other three nodded their heads in agreement. But Duke noticed a hesitation in his sidekick's expression.

That's right, his parents, realized Duke.

The bounty hunter placed his hand on Ishiro's shoulder.

"Tell them to come with us," Duke said.

Ishiro'shea sprinted back into the war room but returned mere moments later. He simply shook his head.

"Yeah, I had a feeling they would stay. At least we know someone with a brain will be in that room," Duke said, smiling.

Ishiro'shea nodded again and gave Duke a thumbs-up.

"Let's go."

***

The *Deus Ex Machina* had been protected from the attack of the Cosmoses in the base's underground docking port. It cruised through a long, well-lit tunnel and emerged into the Irish sky a few blocks away from the base's location. As it turned around, the carnage from the three Cosmoses came into clear view. The city was on life support, and the life support was also on life support.

The defense force that was nearby was making no headway. On the outskirts of the city, an entire legion of cube tanks had melted down from the acidic spit of the Underlord, creating a lagoon of liquid metal and twisted steel. The Aqua Demon was wrapping its long neck around the handful of erect buildings, then tightening its grip until the structures caved in on themselves, like a boa constrictor wrapped around a tube of brittle crackers. The air strikes were nearly nonexistent as every wave was mowed down by the Winged Death's eye beam or midair kicks from its horse-like lower body. Ships would simply explode like some sort of gruesome fireworks display when the massive hoof of the space centaur connected. It was a massacre.

"Are we going to engage?" asked Lilly.

"No," replied Duke quickly. "We aren't going to fall into the same trap as the Earthers. We're better than that. No offense to your parents, Ish."

The ninja did not turn around from the navigational panel. He kept plucking away at the various buttons and levers and dials.

The *Deus Ex Machina* quickly decreased its altitude and zipped into the remains of New Tokyo. The Cosmoses were still busy with the Earth forces, though it seemed that the influx of monster fodder was slowing a bit. Someone had to see that these amounted to nothing more than suicide missions. The ship breezed over fallen structures and entire blocks engulfed in flames before approaching the remains of the industrial sector.

"At least the Cosmoses seem to be ignoring this part of town," said Po'l.

"Probably because they've already flattened it," added Lilly.

"It should buy us some uninterrupted searching time to find these bastards," chimed in Duke. "And that's the best news we've had in a while."

The *Deus* continued to skim the remnants of the sector. With so much of the area being mauled into an unrecognizable mound of scrap, the Yehaso would have a ton of hiding places and cover. Even the downed escape vessel would be tough to spot in the carnage. The only areas that were fully exposed were the flattened tracks left from the Cosmoses.

And that's where they were.

Got ya.

In what appeared to be a flipper print from the Aqua Demon, there sat the boxy shuttle craft. The side door was ajar and a ramp extended from the ship to the ground. The three Yehaso stood at the bottom of the ramp, huddled so close together so that they looked like a single being.

The *Deus* decreased its altitude and dipped to the left until it almost touched the Irish soil about ten city blocks from the stranded alien trio. The *Deus* remained hovering, behind the remains of a toppled office building. Despite the ample camouflage, Duke and crew kept visual contact with the Yehaso.

"Did they see us, Ish?" asked Duke.

The ninja shook his head.

"Good," replied the Nova Texan. "Now we just need to hop out and grab 'em. Easy."

Lilly cleared her throat, causing Duke to look in her direction.

"Yes, Lilly?"

"If we're right and they *are* tethered to the monsters, I'm not sure grabbing them is going to do much," the Gartoshian began. "I think we should avoid the hopping out part and just get right to the blowing them up bit."

She's right, thought Duke.

"Well, okay. All in favor of letting loose the fury of the *Deus*, raise your hands," said Duke.

All four crew members raised their hands. Before their arms lowered, Ishiro'shea had the ship above the debris with a direct line of sight to the Yehaso.

And another ship.

A ship Duke recognized. *Mazilda*.

CHAPTER 34

SURRENDER

"SHIELDS UP, ISH," SCREAMED DUKE. "Hurry—"

The *Deus Ex Machina* was rocked by a round of piercing laser blasts from Mazilda's vessel. The aging ship regained stability, as did its crew.

"Are the shields operational?" shouted Duke.

Ishiro'shea extended a thumbs-up.

Another volley of artillery crashed into the *Deus*. The shields turned what would have been another rocking into more of a wobble.

"Her ship was a lot less scary when I was the size of a space monster," Duke moaned.

A third barrage connected.

"So, are we going to, you know, fire back?" chirped Po'l.

"We can take a few more hits. Aim our attack on the Yehaso. Let's kills these assholes," ordered Duke.

But the ship didn't fire. Instead, Ishiro'shea turned around from the panel and shrugged his shoulders.

Duke's eyes darted to the view screen. Under Mazilda's ship was the damaged shuttle craft. But the Yehaso weren't there.

"She already has them!" yelled Duke. "Send everything we got at Mazilda."

The *Deus* unleashed every weapon that it had at its disposal. Laser pulses. Cannons. Explosive projectiles. All aimed at the enemy craft. Within moments, the entire theater of battle was covered in an opaque cloud of smoke. What wasn't rubble was now rubble; what was rubble was reduced to micro-rubble; what was micro-rubble was simply evaporated into nothingness. The *Deus* maintained its steady bombardment for a full ten minutes. There was no return fire from Mazilda's craft.

"They couldn't have survived that," exclaimed Po'l. "There's no way."

"But did they escape? I couldn't see anything in this mess," replied Lilly. "Mazilda is pretty crafty."

Ishiro'shea pointed to the view screen. The dust was slowly separating into a translucent haze. There was Mazilda's ship. It wasn't destroyed. But it didn't seem to be doing too well either. It was grounded, covered with the remnants of a parking structure. A few of the exterior lights blinked.

The *Deus Ex Machina* approached the downed ship cautiously. It touched down a mere city block from Mazilda.

Duke stood up from his captain's chair. He straightened his posture.

"Ishiro'shea," he began, formally, "focus attack on the wounded craft. Destroy it."

"Do you want to hail her?" asked Lilly. "Make sure the Yehaso are in there?"

Duke didn't acknowledge the Gartoshian's query.

"Fire!" he commanded.

Goodbye, Mazilda.

The ninja began the assault. All visible parts of Mazilda's ship began to erupt in explosions. The attack would need to be a swift one as the structural integrity of the craft was already beginning to falter.

Suddenly, Duke was thrown from his feet by a massive tremor. Then a second. Ishiro'shea was catapulted from the control panel to the other side of the bridge unceremoniously.

"What was—" began Duke. He didn't finish his sentence. The forward screen was completely engulfed by a giant flipper. "Pull back! Pull back now, Ish!"

The ninja sprinted to his seat and the *Deus* was airborne in an instant. As the ship reversed through the decimated industrial sector, all three Cosmoses came into view. They all three created a titanic barrier between the *Deus* and Mazilda's ship.

"Duke," began Lilly, "looks like Mazilda is hailing us."

Mazilda's face took up nearly the entire screen. Behind her was the cyborg. His half-metal face was smirking. There was also a brutish Jungafallowian, a blubbery Tardasian, and a rather bland and insignificant looking Four I's officer.

"Hey there," she began. "Ishiro, nice to see you. And you other two."

Lilly and Po'l did not respond though Duke could hear the Gartoshian growl through gritted teeth.

"Let's not drag this out," Mazilda continued. "If you surrender, I won't kill you. We can call it even for all of the other stuff that's transpired."

"Even? You killed the man who raised Ishiro. Remember that? Oh yeah, and you nearly ended the existence of our universe," replied Duke.

"You don't really have much of a choice, LaGrange," interjected the Tardasian. He looked a lot like Duke's former colleague, Sol, but even more disgusting.

"Before you say anything Duke, you know he's right," Mazilda confirmed. "You don't have much of a choice. Even though it appears that you've figured out that they were our spies, we have the Yehaso. Safe and sound."

"Yes. Your spies," Duke responded. "Clever."

She doesn't know we know about the connection to the monsters, thought Duke.

"And the three Cosmoses will squash you and your ship at our command. Our sophisticated mind control device implants worked to perfection," said Cloax. "This was a rather easy takeover, giant monster fights notwithstanding. Earth's defenses were somewhat exaggerated."

"You got us. Mind-control implants. Super clever," Duke retorted.

"I sense you aren't taking this seriously, Duke. You don't think I will kill you? You should know better by now," Mazilda replied. Her eyes tightened and a tinge of red peeked through to the surface of her jaundiced skin.

Duke did not respond.

"Fine," she huffed. "Send them in, Rozz."

Within a few moments, the forward screen of the *Deus* began to beep.

"Look at your scanners," Mazilda said, smiling. "What do you say now?"

The screen was detecting the presence of a substantial fleet hovering over their current location, just above the heads of the Cosmoses.

"More ships? Neat. You do know that if you are just going to kill us, three cosmic monsters will probably do the trick," Duke smirked.

"Why are you pissing her off?" whispered Po'l. "Shouldn't we surrender and fight another day, or at least have the hope to fight another day?"

Duke let out an audible groan.

He's right.

The bounty hunter faced the screen.

"Fine, you win. We give up. We will take the deal and be your prisoners," Duke said, raising his hands in the air signifying his submission.

"Ish, set us down," commanded Duke.

Mazilda's face relaxed.

"I'm glad you are making this easy. I know our history doesn't mean much now but I am truly happy that I don't have to kill you. And Ishiro," said Mazilda. "Just so you don't try anything, you four meet us out in front of your ship. Az and Darfol-Chell will be out there to escort you into the *Starsplitter*. Leave your weapons on board. If we even *think* we see Betsy, you will all be flattened."

Duke nodded. Mazilda cut transmission.

"So do we go out guns blazin'?" asked Lilly.

"No, I don't think so," Duke answered. It was clear that Lilly, Po'l, and Ishiro'shea were caught off guard by the bounty hunter's response. "No. Not yet, at least. Let's see what this does first."

Duke pointed to the captain's chair. On the left armrest was a plastic dome. Inside the casing was a red button. He sauntered to the chair, opened the hatch, and pressed the button. He then looked at his three friends and tipped his hat in each of their directions.

CHAPTER 35

TETHERED

"**I** DON'T WANT TO QUESTION your decisions, fearless leader, but do you think it's wise to keep them alive?" whimpered Redd. "They've been known to pull fast ones on everyone. Not that you would fall prey to their tactics."

Mazilda was sliding her throwing daggers into the sheath on her hip but paused abruptly when Redd finished his query. She looked at him, tilted her head, and squinted.

The sweat trickling down the Four I's officer's forehead picked up speed until it could more aptly be described as a raging river.

"I'm sorry, Mazilda. I didn't mean to question—" he stammered.

"Don't worry about it. It's a fair question," she replied, her lips turning upward.

Redd Warwick exhaled.

"You see, when Duke captured me at Joe's, I wanted them to kill me. But no. They left me on Psitakki, in the company of the Chief Interrogator General. That wasn't a pleasant time in my life, Redd. Understand?" she asked.

"Yes, m'am," the officer replied, bowing.

"I am going to return the favor. Duke and his friends are going to suffer. A lot. For a long period of time. But, unlike me, they will never escape. I will find the most ruthless torture chamber in the cosmos that will make the Chief's dungeon seem like a day spa, complete with cucumber water and herbal scrubs. So I was *hoping* that they would surrender," Mazilda concluded.

Az, Rozz, and Darfol-Chell chuckled in the background.

"And what about Earth?" asked Redd.

He sure is full of questions today, thought Mazilda.

"Earth? We do what we were told to do with it. Destroy it. Let these three monsters and the Yehaso do their thing. Right?" Mazilda turned to the three aliens. They all nodded in agreement. "Now if you don't mind, Redd, let's go rid the universe of its greatest nuisance."

Redd bowed.

Rozz walked over to Mazilda, his stench preceding him.

"Good news, Mazilda. The *Starsplitter* is operational. At least, it will get us out of here. The weapons are down. The shields are down. But it will go."

"That's fine, Rozz. We have all the escort we need. If Earth has any more forces, they will be crushed by the Cosmoses or picked off by our fleet. The scanners haven't picked up anything from neighboring systems so our entire armada should easily get out of here and leave the monsters to end the existence of this miserable planet."

The *Starsplitter*, despite being roughed up considerably by the *Deus*, looked fairly unscathed on the interior. The hallways had a few exposed wires and a blinking light here and there, but overall not bad. Mazilda, Az, Rozz, Darfol-Chell, and Redd Warwick made their way through countless corridors until they reached a cargo door in the underbelly of the ship. They were met by a dozen Four I's soldiers.

"If you see anything unusual, open fire," she commanded the leader of the squad.

"Affirmative," he replied.

She peered over and noticed Venksplin, Sattlamora, and Lantejira.

"You three can come if you want or watch from the ship. It should be relatively quick," said Mazilda.

"We will remain here, if it's all the same," Venksplin replied.

Cowards.

The cargo doors slid open and a long ramp descended from the ship to the ground. The five crew members made their way to the flattened bit of New Tokyo landscape, followed closely by the Four I's security detail. They fanned out immediately, creating a semicircle around Mazilda and her team.

The ramp was already extended from the *Deus Ex Machina*, though Duke nor any of his compatriots were visible.

"You see 'em?" asked the Darfol head of the Jungafallowian bruiser. "They better come out here."

Mazilda and the team made their way until they were less than a shuttle craft's length from the *Deus'* ramp. She raised her right hand and everyone halted. Mazilda pivoted toward the soldiers and looked skyward. Standing above her were three titanic space monsters creating a makeshift skyline of New Tokyo. She smiled. She looked back at the *Starsplitter*. She could barely make out the six eyes of the Yehaso, hiding safely in the cargo bay.

The plan worked, she thought.

"They could be preparing for a last stand, a foolish one, but one nonetheless," advised Az.

"Yes, they could blast us away with the ship's cannons," responded Rozz. "The more I think about this, this isn't the strongest of plans, Mazilda."

"Shut up, you idiot. Trust me. He will come. They will come. They will surrender," she replied. "Duke LaGrange thinks that as long as he's alive, the universe has a chance. He talks so much about hope that you'd think he actually believes it. I know he expects his followers to believe it. He's *that* arrogant. That ignorant. He won't make a last stand and let Earth and the rest of the universe be without their precious Nova Texan savior. And he doesn't understand our role in this whole ordeal. He thinks we are just thugs. Low-level criminals. He has no idea of the scope of every-thing—the magnitude of what we are doing and the insignif-icance of his own existence."

"But one shot and we're dead," chimed in Rozz. "He could take off and be gone."

"And then he is destroyed by the Cosmoses, by our fleet. He doesn't want that. Like I said, he believes that they can't beat us without his assistance," Mazilda explained.

Mazilda turned back around to face her former love's aging spacecraft. The ramp had ascended back up into the bowels of the ship.

Interesting move, Duke. New tricks? Mazilda mused.

"Now what?" asked Az.

Mazilda pondered her next steps hard but not long because her train of thought was quickly interrupted. A loud explosion came from behind the *Starsplitter*. Then another. It was the Winged Death, and it was hurling eye lasers at their ship. It was rocked. Explosions lit up the upper hull. The three Yehaso were thrown from inside the cargo bay; all three tumbled down the ramp, hitting the soil with a thud. A ball of flame engulfed the ship, courtesy of the Aqua Demon. The Yehaso scurried to Mazilda and her crew.

"What's going on with the Cosmoses?" she screamed at Venksplin.

"We have no idea," he replied. "They aren't responding to us."

"Our tethers are cut," cried Sattlamora. "The communication link is out."

"This has never happened," added Lantejira.

The Underlord hurled his toxic sludge at the *Starsplitter*, covering it completely. The venomous liquid quickly ate away at the burning ship. The once impressive vessel now began to collapse in on itself. Before Mazilda could blink, it was nothing more than a few mounds of melted scrap.

Mazilda tried to collect herself. She pointed to the Four I's security lead.

"Try and take down that ship. Go now!" she barked. The dozen or so soldiers sprinted toward the *Deus*, firing off their guns with reckless abandon.

It took a single blast from the *Deus Ex Machina* to wipe the entire security detail from the face of New Tokyo.

Damn.

Near the smoldering remains of the *Starsplitter*, Mazilda noticed something less mangled than everything else in her view. The damaged escape pod.

"Az, any chance you can get that thing flying?" Mazilda asked the cyborg, pointing at the shuttle craft.

"One of the thrusters is still working, or it was when we scanned it upon arrival. The Yehaso just didn't know how to fly it properly," Az replied.

"Let's go," she said motioning to the team.

The door was still open to the shuttle and they piled in.

"There won't be room for us all," noted Rozz.

"Yes there is," Mazilda replied matter-of-factly. "These three aren't making the trip."

The Yehaso all froze, their expressions identical.

"But—" began Venksplin. The shuttle craft door closed on them.

The ship's engine started and it skipped away through the ruins of what was once downtown New Tokyo.

"Why did you leave them?" asked Redd.

"You want to trade places with them?" replied Mazilda.

"Well, no—"

"Then shut up. They will be fine. They have three giant monsters to protect them, remember?" said Mazilda.

The shuttle bobbed and weaved amidst the three Cosmoses obliterating what was, until moments ago, Mazilda's formidable armada and escort off of Earth. Now, instead of the firepower of the Cosmoses providing cover for escape, it was the destruction of Mazilda's fleet and the ensuing chaos that gave the escape pod an opening to depart the crazy blue planet. They picked up speed and exited the atmosphere as the creatures continued to overwhelm the Four I's force.

CHAPTER 36

THANK YOU, BIG RED BUTTON

"WHAT I DON'T UNDERSTAND, DUKE, is how this whole linking thing works," said Po'l. "I mean, if the Yehaso and the monsters are linked, how did the ship cut that off? I mean, it's more than just talking back and forth; we saw that they were linked biologically. When one was drunk, the other was. I just don't get it."

"Your guess is as good as mine," replied the bounty hunter, shrugging his shoulders. "All I know is that those monsters are ripping Mazilda's armada to shreds."

"But where's Mazilda?" chimed in Lilly.

Duke shrugged his shoulders again.

"You think she got away?" asked Po'l.

"Probably," Duke replied. "She's a survivor. She escaped Psitakki, didn't she? But, as much as it pains me, this isn't about her. I'm not sure what she's up to or why she's still fighting this fight after LePaco was killed, but the ones who we need to find are the Yehaso. We get them, we save Earth. That's our mission. But...we also don't want to find them until these monsters take out all of Mazilda's fleet."

"I think that's a done deal, Duke," answered Lilly. "There isn't a single Four I's ship in the air. They crushed them all. Every last one of them. Gone. And the big bug is back underground somewhere. The Aqua Demon is already in Dublin Bay. The flying one is just hovering above us, like it's suspended from a ceiling."

Ishiro'shea raised his hand, signaling the attention of the crew. He pointed to the forward view screen. The screen zoomed in on an area near the remains of Mazilda's ship.

"There you are, you alien bastards," exclaimed Duke.

The Yehaso weren't hiding. They were waving their hands frantically in the air and appeared to be shouting at the Cosmoses.

"I think they're just as confused as us," said Duke. "I doubt they know why their control of these brutes has been temporarily suspended."

"But it's temporary," Lilly reminded the crew. "If we don't get rid of them now, they will regain control and we're back where we were—minus Mazilda, of course."

"All we need to do is kill them, then. So Ish, lock in the targets," Duke ordered.

The ninja extended the all-too-familiar thumbs-up.

"You're welcome, Earth," said the Nova Texan. "Again."

Nothing happened.

"Ish?"

The ninja kept plugging away at the control panel, shaking his head.

"I think the weapons aren't functioning," said Lilly. "I didn't think we took that much damage."

"Keep trying, Ish," said Duke. "I have no idea what's going on. Maybe the *Deus* can't keep the communication between the Yehaso and Cosmoses severed and fire our weapons? I really have no idea anymore. It's not even worth guessing what this ship is thinking. It calls Blops on the phone one day, the next day it's talking to monsters. I really need to learn to speak—"

The bounty hunter was cut off by the seismic rumble of the Winged Death landing nearby. On the screen, they could see the Yehaso being thrown into the air and deposited in a mound of dirt at the edge of the giant flipper print. The Winged Death knelt down and swiped its massive hand near the Yehaso's location. Its claws dug into the earth and closed, encapsulating dirt, debris, and presumably, the Yehaso. It leapt into the air and headed towards Dublin Bay.

"They got their connection back," shouted Duke. "They're escaping!"

"Do we go after them?" Po'l asked.

"And the Underlord just reared its ugly head. It's on a cliff overlooking the bay. And the Aqua Demon surfaced. It's right below the bug," observed Lilly.

"This is not good. Not good at all," said Duke.

The Winged Death whizzed past the Underlord, at the very edge of the cliff, then halted and turned to face the gargantuan insect. It extended its arm and the giant bug let loose a stream of its acidic spit. It hit the Winged Death directly in the hand—the hand holding the Yehaso. Simultaneously, the Aqua Demon hit the flying monster's hand from the other direction with a blast of fiery breath, covering the flying beast's entire arm in flames.

Maybe the ship didn't lose a connection, realized Duke. *The Winged Death is letting them do this to his arm.*

The Winged Death went limp midair and fell into the bay below. The Underlord froze, then tumbled from the edge of the cliff into the choppy waters. The Aqua Demon's long neck flailed for a moment, then it sank underneath the water's surface.

The Cosmoses were dead. The Yehaso were dead.

Duke collapsed into his captain's chair.

"Thank you, big red button."

CHAPTER 37

FROM EARTH TO KELT

T HE MILITARY BASE AT NEW Tokyo had remained intact, for the most part. Duke, Ishiro'shea, Lilly, and Po'l entered and were met with a round of applause from the officials still there. General Munger was the first to approach the crew. She saluted them all and smiled. Colonel Tott stood behind her; he grimaced, more hostile in appearance than normal. He raised his hand to his forehead in what Duke assumed was the quickest salute in Earth military history.

"I must say, you were right," began General Munger. "Your theory about the Yehaso was spot-on. I'm glad you pursued it, even without our help."

"Thank you, General. We're also pretty damn happy that we were right," the bounty hunter replied. "I wish it could have been resolved without as much death and destruction, though."

"We are in agreement there, Duke. Thank you again," the General said. She extended a hand. Duke shook it. She then peeled away from the group and began directing her subordinates who were still in the heat of battle.

Duke extended a hand to Colonel Tott. The Colonel simply snarled and followed the General.

"I love you too, Colonel," smirked Duke. He turned to face his crew members, "What an ass."

The Father and Yumi entered the room. Yumi ran to her son and embraced him. The Father followed suit. Pretty soon, Duke, Po'l, and Lilly were also receiving hugs from Ishiro's parents.

"It looks like we owe you again," the Father said to Duke.

"Well, you owe *us*," Duke corrected him. "But I wish we would've been able to take out Mazilda too, once and for all. There's something not right about this entire ordeal. I just can't put my finger on the 'why.'"

"If anyone can get to the bottom of it, it's you. All of you," exclaimed Yumi.

"And I guess you won't come with us?" asked Duke.

The Father and Yumi looked at each other and smiled.

"No, this is our home. We almost had it in pretty good shape before the Yehaso. I think we can do it again," answered the Father. "The people of Earth got a brief taste of what we *can* be. I think that will drive them to achieve it once again."

"Barring any more attacks from cosmic monsters," Yumi added.

"I hope the next time we see you, it will be on a Daedean beach or a cave on Oscavia," said Duke.

"Or a bar on Kelt," jested Yumi.

Duke laughed. "I knew I liked you."

"Next stop, Kelt. Cyborg Joe's," shouted Duke from his captain's chair on the *Deus Ex Machina*.

Ishiro'shea extended a thumbs-up.

"I could use a drink," gasped Po'l.

"Cheers to that," replied Lilly.

The voyage through the warp station to Kelt was a painless trip. A much-needed painless trip. It was a pleasant sight when Kelt came into view on the forward screen.

"Are you going to stay for a bit, Duke? Enjoy some much deserved downtime?" asked Po'l.

"As much as I'd love to, I'll probably just say hi to Earl, have a Glyptodian Summer Ale, and then head back to Neprius. I miss it."

The crew all looked at Duke. Mouths agape.

"Yes, I know, I know. I miss Neprius," he said submissively. "I also miss Ja'a. And *my* bar. It's not Cyborg Joe's, but it ain't half bad. It's getting some good reviews."

They all laughed until Po'l shot down the merriment with a single question.

"*How* are you getting back to Neprius?" asked the former Neprian freedom fighter.

The bridge went silent.

Duke cleared his throat. "So the plan is...you see...I don't really..."

"I will help him with that," boomed a voice from seemingly out of nowhere. Its cadence was the speed of especially thick syrup on a shallow incline.

"Who in the—" began Po'l.

"Oh sorry, I keep forgetting to say hello first," the voice continued. "Hold on."

Materializing on the bridge next to Lilly was a diminutive mound of fleshy, half-digested marshmallows.

Blop, a Blop from Blop.

"Good to see you again," Duke said with a nod.

"And you as well. Very good job defeating the Yehaso and their monstrous counterparts," Blop said.

"Yeah, about that. It wasn't exactly what you led me to believe our mission was," Duke replied.

"Nor was it what we thought it was. Something is going on in this universe. Something big. Something that might even be beyond our ability to ascertain. We did not anticipate, nor did we figure out, the Yehaso's plan until you did. That is quite strange because, as far as this universe goes, we usually have a pretty good handle on everything. That's why we like this one so much."

"What do you mean? You just thought it was an attack on Earth from Mazilda?" asked Duke.

"Yes. We knew Earth was important—rather, *is* important—for the survival of the universe," said Blop.

"Come again?" interrupted Lilly.

"You will have to trust me on that fact, my Gartoshian friend. But what I don't understand is who or what summoned the Yehaso. We knew very little of their species. Someone that has extremely deep knowledge of this universe and others, I presume," said Blop.

"I think the Yehaso are officially extinct now," Duke replied.

"Possibly," began Blop. "If you believe their stories. I have a feeling that we might see them again. Somewhere."

Great, thought Duke.

"So this mysterious entity with the deep knowledge, do you think they also aided LePaco and caused the war?" asked Duke.

"Maybe. Or it could simply be coincidence. He was pretty insane, after all," Blop said. "However, I do think Mazilda will lead you to answers. That was very intelligent of you to let her escape."

Duke looked at Ishiro, fighting off a burst of laughter stuck in his throat.

"Yes, it was all part of our plan," Duke replied, partaking in an exaggerated bow.

"Very good. We do have a read on where they were heading—" Blop began before being interrupted by Duke.

"Sorry to cut you off, Blop. But I'm out. I'm sitting this mission and any future missions out. I just want to go back to Neprius. Go back to Ja'a. I've done my part. I don't want Mazilda to ruin my life anymore than she has. I figure I only get one—I'm not as lucky as a Blop in that regard—and I want to spend it with Ja'a. On that primitive rock that I, for some reason, now love."

Blop stood there motionless, his large eyes blinked. After an age, the silence was broken.

"Very well. I will take you to Neprius," Blop said. "We have constructed a portal station behind a dead planet not far from here. It will connect you to Neprius. It is the only connection point in existence, but it is stable. It is time for Neprius to introduce itself to the rest of the universe, I suppose."

CHAPTER 38

SURPRISE

QUEEN JOE'S HAD CLOSED FOR the night, so the bar was empty minus Duke, Ja'a, and a few of their closest friends.

"That's about it," finished Duke, as he brought a cold mug to his lips.

"Interesting," replied Vernglet Wip, tapping his long, skeletal fingers on the bar top.

"Very," huffed the barrel-chested Bu'r, staring into a glass half filled with golden ale.

Ja'a got up from the barstool and walked behind the counter. She started to clean some of the glasses.

"Ja'a?" asked Duke.

"Yes?" she replied.

"Do you have any thoughts?" the bounty hunter asked.

"I do. I always do. Part of me is excited that we now can meet our neighbors in the universe. I know there is good and bad that comes with that. I mean, just think of our limited interaction with the rest of the universe already. We got both Ot Vangu and Duke LaGrange," she stated.

"I better be the 'good' part of that combo," said Duke.

Ja'a simply smiled.

"For our planet, we are still restoring peace and prosperity from the cycles of turmoil. It's a lot to ingest and analyze," she continued. "I am torn. I need time. But there is one aspect that I don't need time on."

Duke's eyebrows raised.

"And that is?" he asked cautiously.

"Why are you here?" she snapped.

"Excuse me?" Duke retorted.

"Why are you here and not out with your friends tracking down that crazed bitch? You need to finish what you started, Duke LaGrange, and you need to save the universe once and for all." Duke was motionless as if he had been welded to the barstool. "You trust Blop, right?" she asked.

"Yes, but—" Duke began.

"But nothing," Ja'a interjected. "Duke, I love you. You are more important than anything to me. But just as you gave me *my* freedom to build a better Neprius, I know you need the freedom to save the universe. That's your destiny."

"But—" Duke began again.

"So get in that rusted tin can of a ship, go get Ishiro, go get Lilly, and go get Po'l, and whomever else you need and help us create a better universe. A better universe that Neprius is now going to be a part of. A better universe that our child is going to be part of."

Duke dropped his glass of Glyptodian Summer Ale.

Ja'a smiled. Vernglet and Bu'r both burst into laughter and embraced the bounty hunter from each side.

"Congratulations," they both shouted in unison.

Duke never took his eyes off of his beautiful partner.

The front door burst open, jarring the bounty hunter out of his daze. Po'l and Lilly ran over the threshold, shouting "Surprise!" The Father, Yumi, and Earl followed. Then Yeop. Blop, a Blop from Blop slowly entered. Lastly,

Ishiro'shea strolled into Queen Joe's. He looked around, taking in the surroundings. He then gave Duke a thumbs-up.

All of the people that meant something to him were now in the same place. At the same time. In his wildest dreams, he would never have thought this possible.

Duke locked eyes with Ja'a. She was truly the most special person in the whole of the universe. And she would be the most wonderful mother in the universe; all he had to do was save it. Again.

THE END

I hope that you enjoyed *How to Battle Giant Monsters with a Drunk Space Ninja*. If so, I'd love for you to join my newsletter at DukeLaGrange.com.

Stay tuned for the continued Adventures of Duke LaGrange, or check out The Adventures of Duke LaGrange Omnibus, which includes special features and an exclusive bonus chapter!

ABOUT THE AUTHOR

©JAY KEY 2018

JAY KEY knew at a young age that he wanted to be the world's first professional wrestler turned fraternity president turned digital media executive turned Society of Vertebrate Paleontology-approved blog writer turned science-fiction comedy author. At various points, Key called Dallas, San Francisco, and Los Angeles home—but it wasn't until a move to Chicago that writing professionally became a reality. Authoring a serialized version of *The Adventures of Duke LaGrange* and a popular blog on the paleobiological accuracy of dinosaurs in pop culture, Key used that momentum to complete *How to Pick Up Women with a Drunk Space Ninja* in 2017. It debuted with Star Wheel Books in 2018.

Jay now lives in a suburb of Dallas-Fort Worth with his wife, Shelley, their daughter, Finley, and their French bulldog, Olive. He is a member of the Science Fiction & Fantasy Writers of America.

facebook.com/starwheelbooks

twitter.com/ofamesozoicmind

instagram.com/jaykkey